THE LAKE POET

Also by Kathy Stevenson

Second Thoughts (Essays)

The Lake Poet

a novel

by Kathy Stevenson

Kathy Stevenson

Thirteenth Angel Press

Wordsworth went to the lakes but he was never a Lake Poet.
He found in stones the sermons he had already hidden there.

Oscar Wilde

The lunatic, the lover, and the poet,
Are of imagination all compact ...

William Shakespeare

For all the women who keep their art in their attics

and

for Joe

The Thirteenth Angel

The thirteenth angel watches over my lover as she writes.
Surrounded by prairie, lost in reverie, her angel eyes reflect
the distance of mid-winter passage in Atlantic storms.

Her face bleached, fractured and cracked by heartland sun;
her wings bored, beaten to splinters by pitiless time.

My lover, the lake poet, sees a world beyond in her face,
a time when passion came home from a long journey,
an age of sacrifice, sacred dances, garlands of ivy and violet.

With her words she cures the plague that is a life
void of heirlooms of the human heart.

Meanwhile, the remaining twelve angels adorn
a grand banquet hall in a prosperous kingdom,
but theirs is another story.

The lake poet describes Zeus and Hera making love
on a golden cloud and how one attending angel
who dared to look was turned to wood
and banished to my lover's imagination.

by Joseph T. Cox

The Lake Poet

by Kathy Stevenson

Prologue

*When my grandmother died last month it was left to me,
her only granddaughter, to go through her private papers.
They were in a small pale blue suitcase that smelled like
musty dreams and promises. The suitcase was locked, and to
unlock it I used a tiny brass key that I remember always
being on a silver chain around my grandmother's neck. When
I was old enough to notice and ask her about the key, she
replied that it was the key to her heart, and left it at that.*

*I didn't know enough to question that statement then, and
as the years went by I forgot about the key.*

*It is possible that you may have heard about my grand-
mother, especially if you live in the Midwest, or perhaps if you
are a scholar of obscure women writers. My grandmother had
a small but devoted following. She was the author of a collection of poems and also wrote a novel called "The Lake Poet"
which enjoyed a brief but intense popularity in the early
1980s when she was nearly seventy-five years old. And, of
course, this past month after her death, the very real possibility of other significant literary works has come to light with*

the revelation that the well known feminist literary scholar Dr. Jane Kendall was named in my grandmother's will as her literary executor.

Together Jane and I have discovered nearly one hundred notebooks filled with jottings of ideas; first, second, and third drafts (and more) of poems and short stories, and at least one more novel, which are threaded throughout the notebooks and will need to be pieced together by Jane. My grandmother also took extensive notes on the books she read, and those notes alone provide a fascinating and illuminating glimpse into what I think of as her soul.

That is what she would like to be remembered for, I believe. She was a wife, of course, and a mother to my mother, but it was books and words and poetry that filled her soul. My mother never understood the selfishness required in claiming that as one's life.

Each summer from the time I was eight, I was sent to my grandmother's from the first week of July until the middle of August. She lived her entire life in Lake Forest, Illinois, a town settled in the mid to late 1800s by a group of wealthy businessmen whose main focus was setting up institutions of higher learning. Also attracted to the area were families who wanted a bit of country to farm or the opportunity to start a small business.

My grandmother had one rule during my visits. I was welcome to stay during those summer weeks, but I could not disturb her work. My mother warned me. Catherine worked on her poetry and writing, and also spent time reading from 8:30 in the morning until lunchtime. After that she was mine. The first summer I visited I thought she would change her mind, and want to play with me all day. In my childish wish to be the most important thing in Catherine's life, I tried to make her see what a desirable companion I was. I fretted and squirmed to get her attention. I made up elaborate plays, dances, and gymnastics routines so that she would not be able to resist me.

"I'll watch you after lunch, Julie," she would say firmly, her hand working her pen over the pages of one of her notebooks. When Jane and I were packing up the notebooks to bring over to the special collections room at Lake Forest College, just holding one in my hand sent me reeling back to those summer days spent with Catherine. The weight of one of her notebooks, the feel of the paper itself, and the smells the paper had absorbed from the house. All of those things...

At the time I had thought it cruel of Catherine to withhold her time, and thus, to me, her affection. To a child, a morning seems like an eternity. Now that I am a mother, though, with two children and a room full of unfinished canvases, I understand her need for solitude and work. I also understand that she was allowing me to become self-sufficient. That plan had never worked with my mother. She just became more needy.

Gradually, over those summers, I looked forward to working beside Catherine, on the screened-in porch on the second story where she worked from June through August. The rest of the year she worked in an upstairs bedroom that she had converted into a writing studio of sorts. The windows of the porch looked out over a canopy of leaves, and over my grandfather's garden, and there it felt as though you were perched in a tree house with a view of the world that no one else was privy to. Sometimes I brought my craft supplies up there, along with books and paper, and each summer as I grew older the morning hours began to disappear more quickly, like sand sifting through your fingers.

During those mornings with Catherine I learned to gravitate toward activities that required solitude. I discovered reading and writing, and I worked on my own amateurish art projects. Occasionally Catherine would glance at something I was working on and she would say something like, "Try to make me see what you see," or, "That is the absolute perfect blue for a robin's egg." I learned from her to listen to the quiet and to see the closest details. Today, in my own work, those qualities have served me well.

I see her poised over her notebook like a small hawk scouting for a place to land. She circles around her writing, comes at it with bursts of true inspiration, and then shapes its nest. When her hand connects with pen, and pen with paper, she is lost to me.

Afternoons were different. After lunch we would go outdoors walking as much as possible. It was the outdoors that inspired Catherine. If she were standing in a copse of trees looking for a red-winged blackbird with her binoculars, she seemed to become one of the trees. I would almost be surprised to see her start walking again; she was so still I would think she had sprouted roots.

Once, in a field of summer flowers on the prairie behind the Shaw house, which is now a retreat for writers and artists, she looked as though she were swaying in the exact rhythm as the joe-pye weeds and prairie grasses that were bending in the hot breezes. I remember the sun on our faces, and her reaching her arms out to embrace it all to her — the sun, the tall grass, the flower crowns. I saw butterflies land on Catherine more than once, and bees would alight on her shoulders but never sting her. By then I was an adolescent, and loved her more fiercely than I loved anything or anyone else in the world.

She could sense that I wanted to learn from her, that my soul was in kinship with hers, and I could tell that it pleased her. "Your mother could never stand still," she told me once. "She would run through the prairie trampling all the plants and scaring every living thing away. Sarah always had to be noticed. She required a lot of space."

We rarely talked about my mother, and my mother rarely talked about Catherine. You could tell that they both might have a lot to say on the subject but were maybe afraid to start talking, because once things are said, it is impossible to get them unsaid.

Nearly all of Catherine's work was done in Lake Forest, although her poems set in Sedona, Arizona, have a certain emotional resonance of their own. My grandmother spent six months in Sedona when she was eighteen. Her Lake Forest poems present charming and evocative representations of Midwestern life and the beauty of the natural prairie setting. Catherine claimed that Lake Forest was wonderfully inspiring because of its place at the edge of a great prairie that gave way to forested ravines, and then opened onto Lake Michigan. That was enough topography to inspire her for her whole life. I had a difficult time developing her eye for the beauty of Illinois. Growing up in the mountains of Arizona, and now living in Colorado, my first impressions of Illinois were that it was flat and one-dimensional. Catherine taught me that the horizon was the thing. She always had her eye on the horizon. In the West, I can't do that. The mountains rise up and hold you there, in that place, at that time.

My grandfather, James Caldwell, was usually at the Inn when I visited. The Forest Inn had been in his family since Lake Forest had started to become more than just a settlement – more of a town with a promising future. His grandfather, Robert Caldwell, had come to Lake Forest by way of the Green Bay trail in 1870, looking for a piece of prairie on which to start some type of business and settle his young family. The first Inn was a small lodging house built in 1875, two blocks south of Deerpath Road and three blocks west of where the train station would be built twelve years later. Robert's wife, Grace Ellen Owens, was from Virginia. Grace Ellen had given birth to three sons, three years in a row, but only one,

John, lived to adulthood. His brothers both died in an influenza epidemic. John attended school at Lake Forest College and then took his place beside his father at the Inn, which by then had moved and become larger. By the time my grandfather, James, who was John's son, had graduated from Lake Forest College, the Inn was a prosperous, established small hotel run by his parents. In 1930, when he was only twenty-five years old, my grandfather built a stately new hotel on its present site on Illinois Road, and took over the running of the hotel.

The Inn burned to the ground in 1938; eight years after my grandparents got married. No one was killed, but the guests, many of them society people there for the "summer season," had to run out into the hot, humid July air clad only in sheer summer nightclothes. Many didn't even have time to put on shoes, and some of the ladies were carried to neighboring homes, so as not to injure their delicate feet.

The Inn was rebuilt from brick and stands today, a magnificent piece of architecture designed in the old English style. Architectural integrity was always preserved during any remodeling, and the Inn today, along with the Presbyterian Church, City Hall, and certain buildings at Lake Forest College, remains elegant and functional.

My grandfather loved the Inn with as much passion as my grandmother loved her prairie, her lake, and her poetry. They never really understood one another's passions but were somehow able to weather forty-five years together. He died at the age of seventy, over twenty years ago.

Now that I think back, I wonder at their relationship. I never saw them kiss, other than a perfunctory peck on the cheek, or show any passion toward one another. They were affectionate as a brother and sister might be. I once asked my mother about this, and she sighed. "That's just the way they were," she said. "Neither one was much for kissing and hugging. Your grandfather spent a lot of time at the Inn. He had his own suite there for the last twenty years of his life, and often spent more time there than at home."

*I guess I had known that, but not really thought about it.
Because by that point my summer visits were over, and I was
removed from those special summers that seemed to exist in a
parallel world.*

*I had an agreement with my mother that I would call her
once I got into Catherine's house. When we were there for the
funeral my mother and Jane and I went through most of
Catherine's things. We didn't go through the few dusty items
scattered about the attic though, and a week ago I received a
note from Catherine's attorney about the existence of a key to
a suitcase that held some private papers. My mother asked me
if I would take care of the matter; she said I was better suited
for the task. I don't know if she had some kind of premonition
that the house held secrets that she would rather not know
about... But that truly is my mother – she is not a woman
who likes looking at the past. Her eyes are always looking to
the future.*

*So the task of visiting Catherine's attorney, Leroy
Jurgensen, fell to me. He would give me the key to the mysterious suitcase. Mr. Jurgensen was ancient; he had known my
grandmother when she was a young girl. His hand trembled
as he handed me the key – a small brass one – the one that I
had seen all those years around my grandmother's neck.*

*The key was so small I barely felt it pressing into my
palm. "Catherine states in an addendum to her will that the
brass key fits a suitcase in the attic," Mr. Jurgensen said. "I
just ran across this last week and realized I hadn't read it as
part of her original will." His eyes were rheumy and wisps of
white hair flew about his gleaming head. "I have no idea
what's in there, of course. Usually they leave some old
mementos or souvenirs..." His train of thought wandered off,
and I began to wonder what I would find.*

*I left the tiny, run-down office in Waukegan's downtown
and headed south on Green Bay Road toward Lake Forest. I
took a left on Deerpath Road and headed east through the
center of town. It was a day my grandmother would have
loved, clear and warm, with the trees in their full summer
glory, and birds soaring high above into the blue. If Catherine
were still alive, I would have taken her down to the lake and
asked her to write the day for me, so that I could hold the
peacefulness to me whenever I needed it.*

*I drove over the railroad tracks, thinking that later I
would have a drink at the Inn, which was now owned by a
consortium of business people. Then I wound my way slightly
southeast, until I came to the white stucco house with the
dark green shutters that was at once so familiar and so mysterious. It was the house where I had spent ten summers, yet
most of the house's history had happened without me. I felt
like an interloper, intruding on secrets, on whispers that still
hung in doorways. Did I really know my grandmother, or did
I just know what she wanted me to know?*

*When I opened the front door, the air inside was warm
and stale, yet I felt an involuntary shiver. I walked back to
the sun porch, where the light was streaming in at a forty-five
degree angle and filled with fairy dust. I wandered from room
to room in a sort of trance, not really wanting to be there
alone, yet wanting to feel every moment fully. Part of me
wanted my mother to be there, helping me with this task, and
I felt tears welling up in my eyes.*

*I walked upstairs to my grandmother's bedroom and over
to the pull cord that opened the panel in the ceiling that went
to the attic. Wooden stairs folded downward and set cleanly
on the floor beneath me. I climbed up into stifling heat to find
the suitcase. I figured there would be old drafts of poems, or
perhaps some of my artwork that she had saved from those
long ago summers.*

Instead there were letters. It looked like nearly a hundred letters, all in the same small ivory envelopes, all addressed in the precise scrawl I knew as Catherine's, and none of them ever postmarked, as far as I could see. They were all addressed to the same person, Mr. Sam Platte of Sedona, Arizona. I knew Sam Platte. He owned the ranch where I was born, and lived until I went away to school. Some of the letters were simply addressed to "Sam," and had no address even. They were all sealed.

I reached my hand deep into the suitcase and gently pulled a letter from the silk lining at the bottom. It was like reaching into a dream and not knowing if what you pull out will be real or just air. The paper somehow felt as familiar to me as my own skin. I opened an envelope that was as fragile as a moth's wing, and read the date on the letter.

September 21, 1929

Dear, dearest Sam...

I quickly set it aside and reached in for another, my hand trembling and my mouth dry.

January 1, 1942

My dear, dear Sam,

All talk is of the war...

I picked up the suitcase and carefully carried it down the wooden stairs, and then downstairs to my grandmother's sun porch. By evening I had organized the letters by date and was ready to read them in order. A cardinal hopped onto the windowsill five feet from where I sat, with a twig of berries in its beak. It tapped the window and then flew away. I read.

September 1, 1929

My dearest Sam,

How can I describe to you the whirlwind of thoughts spinning about in my mind? The autumn leaves outside my window just barely reflect the dizziness I feel inside. You must always remember this: I love you today, and will love you all the rest of my life.

The train ride back to Chicago was uneventful. There were many families returning from summer adventures in the west, but luckily Mother and I had a private Pullman, and we were able to retreat to our compartment when other passengers got to be too talkative and long-winded about their travels. People seem to think that because you are passengers on a train together, you have some sort of bond, and they feel free to hold you captive with their "fascinating" stories of Aunt Mildred's desert cure or their experiences with "real, live Indians."

Of course, we also felt some nervous anticipation about what we might find at home. When we got the telegram at the ranch from Father, the message was so vague we weren't sure how bad things would be. But I am happy to report that Father is doing well. Dr. Harcourt assures us that even though Father suffers from a mild heart problem, he will most likely go on and lead a normal, full life.

Naturally Mother is fussing over him like a hen. She was cossetted by him for several years leading up to our visit to Arizona, so now she must feel as though she is somehow repaying him with her attention. Even though we were only at your family's ranch for six months, I think to Father it seemed much, much longer, as he is unaccustomed to attend-

ing to his own needs. Of course he had Mrs. Haggarty looking in after him, cooking and cleaning up, and doing his
laundry, as she has done for our family for many years. But
he claims that when Mother is absent, Mrs. Haggarty isn't as
meticulous about things. I think he was just lonely for the
unflagging attention Mother gives him.

Mother is doing very well also. I believe the trip to
Arizona did much to improve her health, as it was meant to
do. Dr. Harcourt says that her lungs do seem healthier now,
but that we will need to watch her during January and
February when it is so ungodly cold here.

I think I am the only eighteen-year-old woman to be worried about the health of my parents. As you know they were
married for fifteen years before they had me, and they were
never able to have any other children. So now they are both
in their early fifties, while most of my friends have parents so
much younger!

And of course, your own mother had you well after your
three older sisters were starting into their teen years... So we
are both in similar family situations, with older parents,
except that I've always dreamed of having a sister.

I have decided, dearest Sam, to write you the "normal"
letters of correspondence that a polite young woman would
write to a special male acquaintance, and mail those to you,
as I know your mother will read them. At least that is what
happens here — when I receive a letter from you I am certain
to have to read it at the dinner table to all who are assembled
there. So, I will write you these private letters, as well, letters
with my closest thoughts, and when we see each other next I
will give them to you so that you may read them then and
know the full extent of my love. Won't you be surprised next
summer, when I come out again as we've planned, and I hand
you a box full of letters containing my most private thoughts!

The heart must be a resilient muscle indeed as mine
would surely be shattered into a million pieces right now due

to its longing and yearning to be beating next to yours. I think of so many things we shared; I find it difficult to concentrate on anything else. Mother says I'm walking around with my head in the clouds, but I don't feel that way. I have a very clear vision of what I would like, and that is to be with you.

I wonder if we see the same clouds? I will go outside and demand that the air currents change direction so that my clouds will fly over you, and drop some raindrops on you to remind you of me. Remember the hayloft during the thunderstorm?

Remembering, Catherine

September 9, 1929

Dearest Sam,

I hope you are missing me as I am missing you. I feel terribly lonely, but knowing you must be going through the same thing makes it more bearable. I never dreamed I could be so honest with a person, as I am with you. I don't feel any need for the subterfuge and flirtatious games that I was raised to take refuge in when mingling with the opposite sex. You and I have shown that two adults (yes, I think of us as adults) can be direct and open about their true feelings, and I believe sincerely that that is the best way to be. Things are changing slowly for women and men both; I herald the day when the sexes don't have to play silly mating games, choreographed in a parlor, under the watchful eyes of parents, siblings, and other relatives.

Of course, here in Lake Forest, in 1929, things are still quite provincial. I was just reading an article about a woman novelist who moved by herself to Paris — and she is living quite the scandalous life there. How do some people have the courage to just decide to go to Paris or Italy and write? Something holds me back from such adventures: duty (and love, of course) for Mother and Father; but even if I can't travel far, nothing, simply nothing will keep me from writing. I don't have to be in Gay Paree! I will write good poetry right here, on the edge of the prairie. There are beautiful sights here that the world should know about, and shall!

Speaking of parlor games, I feel I must mention that James Caldwell has been courting me every single day since I've been back. I think I told you about him and his intentions. His family has owned the Forest Inn, here in town, since 1875, and he seems determined to marry me. Mother is also determined to fan the flame of his interest, even though she must sense the strong feelings you and I developed over the summer. I can't be rude and tell him that I love someone else, yet I want to scream every time I see the insipid adoration in his eyes. Adding to Mother's efforts, my best friend Margaret is also conspiring on James' behalf. It seems that over the summer she became extremely fond of one of James' cousins. And she thinks it would be the most fun if we were all one big, happy family.

Why is it that when you try to discourage a man, it often has the opposite effect? Of course, you wouldn't know about that, as I certainly did nothing to discourage you, and we never had to engage in silly parlor games. The open lands were our "parlor," and we had only the quiet, knowing eyes of the owls to chaperone us.

Mother and I are getting a clearer picture of why Father might have suffered from his heart problem. Apparently he invested quite a good sum of money with a company that was developing property in Chicago, thinking that he could make a nice profit when the property was sold off. Unfortunately, the person who was in charge of the company must have taken his investors' money and put it into stocks. Father, of course, didn't know any of this was going on. He just went about teaching his history classes at the College, and heard the news from a friend of his who is a lawyer downtown. Mother is devastated by the news. At this moment she is sitting at the kitchen table, holding a handkerchief and twisting it over and over. Father floats about the house like a ghost, and I sit here wondering what you are doing, and if you are missing me.

I am working on a few poems in the hopes that I will get up enough courage to send one or two of them in to Harriet Monroe's *Poetry* magazine. She has caused quite a stir here in Chicago with her literary publication ever since she founded it in 1912. Perhaps she helps prove that Chicago isn't the backwater town some people think it is. I have read a great deal of the poetry she has published, and I declare that some of my poems are publishable. Am I being too presumptuous? I close my eyes and think of sitting with you at sunset, me reading my poems to you, you with your sketchbook in hand, the smell of the horses and the hay and the dust all so clear to my senses. *All is red, the sky at morning/ the ground I walk on toward you/ where Indians once passed and bled red into the rocks...* Do you remember when I was working on that one?

I am also reading poetry voraciously and trying to memorize as much of it as possible. This helps me to "feel" the poem inside of me, to inhabit the sense of rhythm and language and image that the poem conveys. Memorizing poetry is an exercise Father started me on when I was a very young child. From about age three until about eleven, I loved memorizing poetry; it was a way to get my father's approval. Then from about eleven until about sixteen I had no use at all for poetry — being outdoors and being with my friends was most important. But now that I am a woman of the advanced age of eighteen, I find bits and pieces of poems floating into my head like little baubles floating on water after a shipwreck.

Do you know this one?

> *Our two soules therefore, which are one,*
> *Though I must goe, endure not yet*
> *A breach but an expansion*
> *Like gold to an ayery thinnesse beate.*

This is not one my father had me memorize. It is from a love poem by John Donne, from a volume I discovered one rainy day in Father's library. Some of the sonnets and poems are quite scandalous.

My dearest Sam, I never knew a person could feel such longing and live through it. My heart feels bruised, and my nerve endings are raw even to the pressure of the surrounding air. Are you feeling the same way, or are you too busy with the very real work at the ranch, which I know keeps you occupied from morning until night?

All my love and more, Catherine

P. S. How is the little foal that was born to your mare? Are you keeping him, or are you going to sell him? Keep him for me and we will ride together next spring. Mother and Father can't keep me here once they realize how much in love we are.

September 12, 1929

My dear, dear Sam,

It truly seems impossible that we are on the same spinning planet, wanting to be together more than anything in the world, and yet made unable by our family circumstances to do a thing about it. I tell myself if I had more courage I would get up one morning, announce at breakfast that I was leaving for the train station in Chicago that very day, and jump aboard a train headed toward the western horizon, where my true love waits for me. Our situation is just too difficult. I somehow must find a way to get a letter to you that expresses these true thoughts that I put down to you here in privacy.

We received the letters from you and from your mother yesterday, and that was cause for very joyous feelings on my part, and on Mother's, as she is so very fond of your mother, her old school chum of girlhood days. Isn't it funny to imagine the two of them as they must have once been? I know that my mother rarely laughs as much as she does when she is spending time with your mother. That is one reason I am glad we made the trip to Sedona this past summer.

I spend a great deal of time daydreaming about our time together. I like to close my eyes and start at the beginning, at the train station. When I saw you there, rather dusty and disheveled after your ride, I admit I wasn't overly impressed. I think I was prepared to like you as a sort of cousin, even though we are not related as family. Of course I thought you were very handsome right away, but having no experience in matters of the heart, I didn't really follow that line of thought.

And I thought at the time that you had absolutely no interest in me. You said later that you were instantly struck speechless by my presence, and that your apparent lack of interest was an act because you thought that I had no interest in you! Looking back, I try to find that moment when I knew, the moment when my world turned on its axis and life was different than I ever knew it could be.

That moment came for me when I stumbled upon you down by the barn sketching out the mares. You jumped and shut your notebook when I came close. But then I said I would show you some poems if you would show me some sketches. I remember that exact moment so clearly — the startling clarity of the light, the still hush of the air, the horses' tails twitching hypnotically — it was as though time stopped for an instant, and when it started up again the landscape of my heart was different. One minute I was Catherine, the girl I had always been, and the next minute I was Catherine, who loved Sam.

Perhaps that is what poetry and art try to do — explain the landscape of the heart. I know that when I read a poem that touches me, or look at a painting that stirs something in my soul, I feel changed by that writer's or artist's vision of the world. I don't pretend to understand any of these mysterious feelings, but by the act of creation I believe we try to come closer to understanding what is in our heart and soul.

My dear Sam, I hope you are able to convince your father that you really must attend a university next fall. I think it was a good compromise on both your parts to agree to this one year of immersing yourself in the affairs of the ranch, to see if you are ready to commit to that. But I think that you could gain so much by studying art in a university setting, and by adhering to a schedule that encourages you to produce. I admire your father for not completely forcing the issue; for leaving the year's commitment to ranching open-ended. And I admire you for giving him this year, and postponing your own ambitions. One thing we do have, my darling, is time. After all, we are both young and healthy and we have our whole lives ahead of us. Some days I just want to hug the whole world to me, because life seems so full of possibilities.

I will share with you a little poem that I wrote last night after everyone was asleep. (It is nothing, really, just very simple and in free verse, so don't judge too harshly.)

Fool's Gold

I thought I had put you out of my mind
For a moment, anyway.

But then I looked up
At the crescent moon

It was the curve of your cheekbone.
The stars laughed brightly—
I used to like stargazing
But now all that glitter looks
Like fool's gold.

And the wind, too, was in on the game.
Was it your touch that made the hairs
On my arm stand up,
Or summer's last whisper?

(I never knew there was such a thing as fool's gold until I visited Arizona. There is so much more you need to teach me, and I you...)

Your willing pupil, Catherine

September 13, 1929

My dearest Sam,

I tried not writing to you today, since I just wrote yesterday, but I have this overwhelming need to tell you my heart. You are the only person I can talk to about poetry, creativity, love, and yes, passion. Of course, my best friend Margaret talks constantly of love; she equates it with passion. I think the two can be oceans apart. She fairly gushes forth about her string of infatuations. By the way, she is no longer interested in the cousin of James Caldwell — now she is crazy about a young naval officer from Great Lakes Naval Training Center, which is a few miles north of Lake Forest. Several of us, including Margaret and her officer, went as a group

Saturday to the Deerpath Theatre, where last spring they installed a device for talking pictures. We saw a motion picture called *The Girl in the Glass Cage* starring a young actress named Loretta Young. I thought she was very impressive in her role.

Schools have started this week, and I am feeling a little bit disoriented. Although I could still register at the College for the fall, I believe I will hold to my original plan of starting mid-year. After all, I thought I would be in Sedona with Mother until November, but then when we were called back because of Father's heart problem (which turned out to be minor)... well, then, here I am at sort of loose ends!

Actually, that is not entirely accurate. There is much to keep me busy here — too much, in fact. If I weren't more disciplined, it would be easy to fall into a life that revolves around luncheons, club meetings, and philanthropic pursuits. I actually have to carve out part of each day for reading and writing. Now that I am old enough to accompany Mother on her round of social activities, it would be all too easy to let my more intellectual pursuits drift to the wayside.

For example, just yesterday I attended a book review luncheon with Mother that was sponsored by the Lake Forest Woman's Club. Two women presented essays on the poetry of Yeats while we dined on tomato stuffed with chicken, cloverleaf rolls, and strawberry mousse. Before that we were entertained by a quartet of musicians from the Lake Forest Academy. I'm sure that Yeats himself would have thought the afternoon rather charming but might have been a little taken aback at the depth with which two Midwestern matrons critically analyzed his writings.

Then last night I attended a YWCA meeting at the Gorton School to discuss our chapter's involvement in Hull House. Which will further involve an endless schedule of committee meetings, all of which is for a wonderful cause, but nevertheless left me feeling a bit peevish. A bad trait of mine...

I didn't turn to my reading until I got home, well after ten, and thus I stayed up well past midnight, and am exhausted today. I am reading new poems by Vachel Lindsay (did I tell you I've met him), and I'm reading as much Virginia Woolf as I'm able to get my hands on. She fascinates me — I would like to learn more about her. I wonder if women writers like Virginia Woolf, who have achieved some degree of success and independence because of their literary efforts, know of their impact on those of us who sit at our little desks at midnight scratching out our messages to the world. I wonder how many of us "unknown soldiers" there are who sit alone at night with our thoughts and pens.

Anyway, my dear Sam, all of this goes to prove my point at the beginning of this letter. You truly are the one person I can tell about all of this. I know you feel the same way about your art as I do my poetry. Our endless talks this summer are proof of that. I just have so much more to say, and you are not here to talk to, so this letter, a poor substitute, will have to do.

Yours, Catherine

September 15, 1929

My Love,

How it thrills me to start a letter that way! These letters to you are becoming an important part of my life—a connection to you that I feel as soon as I sit down to write. I can be my true self in these letters, and I can't wait to share them with you when we next meet. It is ever so wonderful to have this secret tucked away inside my heart, but it is also difficult not to shout to the world that I love you and want to be with you every moment of every day. I don't feel the slightest bit odd talking this way to you. Once our love became clear to us, it seemed I was able to freely tell you everything I had kept in my heart for years. I know you feel the same way. I feel like you are the first person to know me on the inside.

As I wrote to you before, that moment when you first showed me your drawings (and thus your soul) was the first moment I loved you. I re-create that morning every day in my mind, because, as you no doubt recall, that was the first time we kissed.

This is how I picture it in my mind's eye: It is late afternoon, and your chores are done. I am on my way to the creek behind the barn when I see you crouched near the corral. You are intent on something; I'm not sure what, or if I should intrude. You are bathed in afternoon light, your tall, lean frame coiled in on itself, on its task. Something makes me move closer, and then closer again. I am near enough to see your dark brown hair lift in the breeze. The breeze also carries your smell to me. How I am suddenly aware of your brown eyes with their flecks of yellow, or the muscles of your arm as it grasps the pencil tightly — I don't know. You have the same eyes and arms you had that morning, but now everything is changed. Now I love you.

But wait. You sense me before you see me, you look up at me, and really see me, and then our eyes meet. I reach my hand out to take your sketchbook, and you hand it to me. The sketches of the mares are more beautiful than anything I have ever seen. I tell you this. You ask about the notebook I have under my arm. I hesitate for a moment — I have never shared my notebooks with anyone.

I tell you I am on my way to the creek. I tell you with a surprisingly calm voice that I will read to you out of my notebook. How can I feel calm? I am in love. I read you poems as the water tumbles by. You listen. We both shiver as the sun goes behind the trees, and we come together as naturally as if we'd known how or why. When neither of us knows anything. Does anyone know?

So, dearest Sam, you know where my thoughts go (and they go there often) when I look toward the west. Every evening at sunset I think of you and wonder if you are perhaps thinking a little of me. Our sunsets here do not compare to your spectacular Arizona ones. Our day's end is more of a fading, or sometimes a curtain closing, rather than a flamingly grand goodbye.

We received your second letter (and your mother's as well), and I was surprised to hear of the trip your father is taking you on. Six months will be a long time to be away. You say you will travel through Arizona south to Mexico, and then actually go into Mexico to see a mining operation being supervised by a friend of your father's. It does sound fascinating, and I wish I could be there with you to see all the marvelous sights.

Traveling by train to the border will be good, because you can make the stops you want to make and see the cattle ranches along the way that your father wants to see. But are you sure that train service in Mexico is so unreliable that you need to travel by horseback once you get over the border? One hears horror stories about Mexico of bandits and general lawlessness reminiscent of the Old West. Please be careful. I couldn't bear it if anything happened to you. This must be the dark side of loving someone — the fear of losing them somehow.

My birthday is in five days, and I'm afraid that Margaret and my mother are concocting some sort of "surprise" party. I dread such things. I don't mind putting together parties for others, but I don't like being the center of attention myself. Luckily there will be enough other women at the "surprise" event who do enjoy being the center of attention, so I should be able to relinquish that role fairly quickly.

I haven't mentioned again the matter of Father's financial problem, but the fact of it has been underlying the normal routines of our lives the past few weeks. Mother seems able to go about planning parties and accepting invitations to everything. She was upset for a couple of days, but then made up her mind not to worry. Father, though, has been very quiet lately, and that is not like him.

Naturally they do not discuss matters of household finance with me, but I have gathered enough from overhearing conversations, and also from Father's melancholy eyes and Mother's forced gaiety. I wish they would be more open with me. After all, I will be nineteen in a few days, and I would like to know exactly what it takes to keep a household going. Many women seem to not want to know; as long as the money is there, they just blithely go about spending it. Then when something happens — death of a spouse, a poor financial decision, illness — they are poorly prepared for dealing with finances. I hope you don't look at this as being a man's realm, because I must tell you I feel very strongly that a woman should be equally aware of these decisions.

How did I start talking about money, and practical considerations, when I should be writing to you about poetry and art? I promise I will devote much space to those two topics next time I write my thoughts to you.

My love comes to you, Catherine

September 21, 1929

Dear, dearest Sam,

Midnight at the end of a very long day. As anticipated, Mother and Margaret did plan a surprise party for my birthday that began at noon—a luncheon and then bridge for about twenty of us. And I hate playing bridge or bunco, or any of the other card games that seem to occupy the time of many women I know. It seems such a waste: well-educated, intelligent women who, in my opinion could be of more use than lunching and playing cards all day. Oh, well, most of them do appear to be perfectly happy; I guess I am the misfit!

Now I sound horribly ungrateful, and perhaps I am. There is just something in me that rebels against a life of frivolity and leisure pursuits. To be sure, most women I know do devote themselves to their families, and they are also tireless workers on this committee to save the world, or that one. (Both valuable and necessary pursuits!) So why do I feel like running out the door and throwing myself into the lake, when I think of such a life? And what do I think I could do that would be any better or more productive?

Questions, questions, my love, but no answers. I would have thought by nineteen, I would have more of a blueprint for my life. Yet, here I sit, mad for no reason, aggravated about people who only wish me well, and wanting nothing more right this minute than to run westward into your arms.

I try to picture myself as a grown-up woman on a ranch like yours, but I wonder if I might be ill prepared for such a life. Your mother runs things so very smoothly — and there is so much she does, and so effortlessly. Her work to me seems much more "real" than the work of the Midwestern housewives with all their latest appliances.

For example, we now own an all-steel refrigerator, and a washing tub called "The Agitator" which actually washes your clothing for you! Mother loves any new household device and claims with every one she purchases that she will be able to cut back on Mrs. Haggarty. But there is a subtle truth to housework: the work itself doesn't actually disappear because of the new machines. You still have to collect the clothes, sort them, put them in the machine, watch it closely in case of malfunction, and then empty it. Mother now has her eye on something they call an electric dishwasher. Father just throws up his hands and doesn't even put up a fight.

Do not ask me how I got sidetracked onto a discussion of appliances. I promise—no more.

People lingered here at the house until late afternoon. It was a very gray and bone-chilling day, so once our guests were by the warm, cozy fire, they hated to leave. By four o'clock my smile began to feel sewn on my face like a rag doll's.

When Father got home he insisted on taking Mother and me and Margaret to the Forest Inn for dinner. He invited James Caldwell and his father to join us for dessert and coffee. I'm afraid I wasn't very good company as by then I had a dreadful headache and my cheeks actually ached from smiling so much. What is wrong with me that I can't appreciate such an outpouring of affection from those who love me most?

James was full of excitement about an idea of his that the Inn will implement beginning October 8th. (Father is very interested in this, because he is an avid baseball fan.) They are going to broadcast every game of the World Series into the Inn's restaurant, hoping to get local people to come out on weeknights and congregate there for dinner. The movie theatre already enjoys tremendous crowds on weeknights. It seems people do not stay home during the week as they once did. I blame this on the popularity of motorcars—we now have nearly two hundred in Lake Forest alone!

My darling, here I meant to tell you all the things I hold dear to my heart (of which you are uppermost), and instead I write of the most mundane aspects of my day. And now it is past midnight, and I am fast on my way to being a twenty-year old matron. Too tired to write any more tonight... I promise my next attempt will be more intellectually stimulating. I crave that communion with you.

Missing you, Catherine

September 25, 1929

My dear, dear Sam,

I imagine you and your father are preparing for your trip south. I hope you will be able to write to me from your various destinations. I will keep writing these letters as well as my "real" ones that I send to you, care of your dear mother. These private ones I will keep safe until I see you this summer. Then you will know just how much I thought of you and missed you during this long separation.

First of all I must talk of poetry. I have been reading madly—all types of poets. I am so glad you love poetry as much as art. I love art nearly as much as poetry, especially your art. I think the two are expressions of life from the same deep well. Some people are equipped to draw from that well and in fact, must draw from it or go mad. You and I are two of those people.

So, here are some poets I have been reading: Amy Lowell, of course (I found some brilliant poems of hers in old copies of *Poetry* at the College). Also Edna St. Vincent Millay—although I myself don't like to write lyric poetry, hers is unique and lovely to read.

Naturally I also like Carl Sandburg because he writes from a Midwestern viewpoint. Also, a Vermonter named Robert Frost is quite good, I think. Is your head spinning yet? I'm not done... I have also discovered these new poets (new to me, anyway). A strange poet named E. E. Cummings (I have to read him several times, and then I think I may understand), Gerard Manley Hopkins, and a Dr. William Carlos Williams. I will copy a favorite poem at the end of this letter (not sure which one yet, so many!) because I know it is more difficult for you to obtain books of new poetry than it is for me.

And these are only a handful of good poets being published today. What this says to me is that there is room for
good writing no matter how many writers are staking a claim.
I just need to be disciplined and persistent. I think (I say this
with some modesty, I hope) that I have some measure of talent. I do believe that some innate talent or gift for the thing
is necessary. But the other traits: persistence, discipline,
luck, fate, timing—all are just as important to an artist's or
writer's career. You will find this out, I think, once you start
sending your illustrations out.

Which reminds me... Can you get your hands on copies
of *Country Gentleman* or the *Saturday Evening Post*? They
often use the most remarkable illustrations by Western
artists, none of whom I might add, are an improvement on
what I have seen of your own work. I've looked at several
back issues at the College library, and in particular there is a
writer named Zane Grey (I remember seeing his books in
your father's office), who often writes for these magazines
and uses illustrations. I think he also uses illustrations in
some of his books. At any rate, perhaps you might send
some of your drawings as samples of your work to Mr. Grey's
publisher.

Wouldn't we have a glorious life together! Myself writing
poetry, and you sketching magnificent scenes of the West.
And the wide-open spaces allowing us freedom to grow.

I wish I could feel the Arizona sun on my arms right now.
It is too dismal here — this has been a wet fall so far, and winter is putting its feelers out already. I close my eyes though,
and I am at our secret spot at Canyon Creek, and the sun is
warming me, and your arms are around me. Delicious... I
love you and miss you and need you to hold me.

Devotedly, Catherine

P. S. Here is an E. E. Cummings poem that is so very

strange, yet I can't stop thinking about his poetry after I read it, and I often have to read it over several times to know why I like it!

in spite of everything
which breathes and moves,since Doom
(with white longest hands
neatening each crease)
will smooth entirely our minds

—before leaving my room
i turn,and(stooping
through the morning)kiss
this pillow,dear
where our heads lived and were.

P. S. again... Do you like it? It is odd, I know, but I think it says the same things the romantic poets tried to say with their language. Perhaps we invent new ways to use language that suit our particular times and our unique souls. Maybe there are many different ways to use language, and we can celebrate the fact that there are differences. I don't think we have to make a choice. I can like E. E. Cummings and Shakespeare and Donne!

September 27, 1929

My dear Sam,

What a lot can happen in just two days. Since I last wrote, Father's financial crisis has revealed itself to be much more serious than either Mother or I realized. He had been trying to keep it to himself, not wanting to worry Mother. And here she was, out blithely buying a new dishwasher on time, and putting on my birthday extravaganza.

Here is what happened. Mother and I came home yesterday afternoon from running errands and found Father sitting at the kitchen table just staring at nothing. When we walked in he didn't say anything — he looked old and frail, much more than his fifty-four years. It took a while, but the truth came out. And you will be proud to know, I demanded to be part of the discussion. At least the part they were willing to reveal while I was there. Who knows what else they talked about behind the closed doors of their bedroom.

To make a long and terrible story short, the investment company we feared invested our money poorly did indeed do so. It seems we are powerless to do anything about it. The person Father entrusted with our money is nowhere to be found, and several other families and individuals are in the same precarious position.

I really don't know how serious this is. As I mentioned before, I have virtually no experience in money matters. The only thing I do know is that I have never seen Mother or Father so upset — not even with illnesses or even the time my mother's sister, my Aunt Lily, divorced her husband because, as she said, "she didn't like the way he chewed his food."

At times like this I wish I had siblings or a close relative, or someone to share this with. I confide in you here, but problems of a family nature are by definition just that. As close as my mother is to yours, the bonds of friendship only stretch so far — she would never reveal the depth of our problems, or their nature. Our family — Mother, Father, and I must sink or swim as one. Right now we are floundering, and I am powerless to help. Even if I tried to get a paying job, it wouldn't begin to help Father replace the savings he lost.

I have never before given much thought to finances. I just assumed we would go on forever as we have. It never crossed my mind that my own circumstances in these matters could change. Naturally, from the volunteer work I have done at Hull House, I have seen extreme poverty, but I always thought those unfortunate people were somehow "different," that they had somehow brought their troubles upon themselves. I had pity, but very little compassion.

My dear, dear Sam... Hopefully by the time you do read these letters, this trying time will be behind us, and I will even be able to smile at how serious I am over our present situation.

Not much to write about poetry. My muse is silent these several days, that part of my brain being taken up with other matters. The most I can do right now is read, and even that endeavor is done halfheartedly and with much wandering of the mind.

By now you are traveling south through Arizona with your father. I fastened a map of North and Central America above my dressing table, (which I have turned, more or less into a desk, not having much use for cosmetics or perfumes), so that I can chart your progress through the southwestern regions of our country, and also through Mexico. How stimulating it must be! In some way it helps me, cheers me even, to know that you are having an adventure. I will somehow share in your travels in my imagination.

Yours, C

October 3, 1929

Dearest,

This past week has been quite trying, due to increasing pressure on Father about our financial situation. But I am sick, sick, sick to death of thinking about all of that, and in this letter I will escape from those pressures and write to you only of things that please me.

First of all, I am reading a new book from the library that

is quite wonderful. It is a translation of the letters of Abelard and Heloise. It reminds me that lovers have loved and been separated through time immemorial, and also that love transcends time and geography. At least these thoughts sound good as I write them to you, but in honesty my heart is breaking from our separation. I miss you, dearest, no less than if I were missing an actual arm or leg. They say that when you lose a limb, you can still feel its presence. The physicality of that feeling describes my missing you.

Oh, how I try from the letters forwarded by your mother to discern some sort of passion, some clue as to how you are truly faring. Is your trip preventing you from thinking of me too much? Or do you see me each night in the moon and stars as I see you? We must talk of these things next time we meet.

Mother just came in and handed me a package from you, postmarked Tucson! I waited until she left the room (surprisingly she allowed me that bit of privacy), and I must thank you, thank you, dear Sam. How did you find this dear little book by Amy Lowell, in Tucson of all places, and then manage to send it back east to Illinois into my hands?

Later: I had to take time away from my letter to read the note you tucked inside the book (at last a note no one else will read but me!) and thumb through the wonderful book that is my "belated" birthday present from you. It's dreadful to think of the family that had to sell all of their possessions by the side of the road, including this precious book, to go further west. But you did find a treasure in among their things. You know that Amy Lowell is one of my favorite poets, and on first perusal *Pictures of the Floating World* looks like it will provide me with many hours of pleasure and study. Thank you, my love. One poem in particular strikes me right away — I had to read it straight through, and then again. And then I had to put the book away for a moment, because the writing pierced me so. It is called

Appuldurcombe Park. Here are the first few lines:

> *I am a woman, sick for passion*
> *Sitting under the golden beech-trees.*
> *I am a woman, sick for passion,*
> *Crumbling the beech leaves to powder in my fingers.*
>
> *The servants say: "Yes, my Lady, and "No, my Lady."*
> *And all day long my husband calls me*
> *From his invalid chair:*
> *"Mary, Mary, where are you, Mary? I want you."*

I have no idea where Appuldurcombe Park is, or who Mary is, but right away I am drawn to Mary and her plight. I wish I could write like that. I will keep trying until I can do something half as good. The most difficult thing is to judge my own work. How do I know when it is good enough? How do you know with your drawings? I know what I like when I read it or see it, but when it comes out of my own head, I find it difficult to be objective.

How I love writing to you about writing poetry. I have no one here to talk to about the creative process. You alone understood this need I have to create, as you have the same need. People who don't have that need go sort of cross-eyed when you try to talk about it. So I just give up.

Reading beautiful words puts me in a mind to create some of my own. And knowing that of anything you could have chosen as a gift, you would choose this small and lovely and cherished book... that makes me love you even more, and hold you even closer to my heart.

As ever, Catherine

P. S. I have read your note about a dozen times already, and am heartened to know that you are as miserable as I am. That sounds awful, doesn't it? That my heart would soar at your unhappiness. I must find a way to write you a note for your eyes only. Perhaps I will send one to your sister Helen, and she could relay it to you. There is some spark in her eyes that belies her motherly reserve, and I feel she would do this for us.

October 31, 1929

My dearest Sam,

They are calling last Friday "Black Friday" in the newspapers, and reading about those calamitous events makes me worry even more about Father and Mother. It is very nearly unbearable here. At least Father has his teaching job, and I truly believe that teachers will always be needed (at least, I sincerely hope so — it would be the blackest days indeed for our country if we started closing our universities).

Meanwhile, here in Lake Forest, everything on the surface appears unchanged. Looking at our local newspaper, you would never know that the country is suffering any kind of economic problems. Instead, the news is of the imminent departures of many families for their winter homes, the incessant bridge and bunco luncheons, and extravagant weddings and dinner parties, which are described in lavish detail. I know we can't be the only family suffering. In fact, another family who invested with the same criminals as Father had to move back to Syracuse, New York, in order to stay with family there. They were left penniless, and have six children.

I imagine you are in New Mexico by now. I hope I will hear word from you soon. I picture the geography in New Mexico to be as stunning as your landscape in Arizona. I would love to see it some day. Will you take me there? I understand that once you are in Mexico, it will be very difficult for you to mail anything, so I may not hear from you for several months. How I will bear not hearing from you, I don't know. My reading and writing continue to save me. When the longing and feelings of intense loss threaten to overwhelm me, I simply force myself to sit down at my desk at the window and take either pen or book in hand. Escaping into that subconscious realm calms me and centers me.

In a black mood to match Black Friday, Catherine

January 1, 1930

My dearest Sam,

Yesterday evening I married James Caldwell in a New Year's Eve ceremony at the Forest Inn. There were nearly two hundred guests. Mother and Father were about to lose everything. I found Father sitting in his study with a small pistol on the desk in front of him, just by chance when I came home early from a meeting one day. I never told Mother. James' family generously insisted on hosting the wedding. No time to write now — leaving tomorrow for Paris. Forgive me.

Yours, as ever, C

January 1, 1931

My dear, dear Sam,

One year has passed since I opened the small blue suitcase where I keep these letters. I believe that I wrote a note the day after I married James Caldwell. And of course, you received the news of my marriage from your mother as soon as you arrived home from Mexico.

My dear Sam, how I wish it could have been different. I can only imagine your shock and pain upon hearing such news. My blood runs cold at the thought, thinking of it even now, one year later.

Since that time, it as if a tornado swept into my life, picked everything up, rearranged it, and dropped me down in a different life.

I have a baby boy, born in November, a perfectly sweet, sturdy bundle we named James, but call Jimmy. I hate to admit this to anyone, but I spend hours gazing at him, trying to memorize every feature on his round little face.

But, I get ahead of myself. You already know about Jimmy, of course, because of the birth announcement that my mother sent to your mother.

Yes, these are things you do know. There are also things you don't know; that no one knows, except for Father and Mother, and I suspect even James, although I hope not.

Our family's situation worsened during November and December of the year before this. James Caldwell continued to call upon me, very insistently, though I assure you, I couldn't have given him less encouragement. (I believe I mentioned him to you once — his family owns the Forest Inn). When he asked me to marry him on Thanksgiving Day (his family invited ours to the Inn for the annual dinner there), I was stunned. Now, upon reflection, I shouldn't have been surprised. But, you will remember, at that time, my thoughts were completely taken up by you.

I will never, never reveal this to anyone else, my dearest Sam. Mother and Father were on the verge of losing everything, including our home. When I found Father that day staring at a small pistol on his desk (that I didn't even know he had), I knew I had to do something. I thought I knew my

father, and it never entered my mind during his financial
troubles that he would hurt himself. I have learned that you
can really never know another person — only what they
choose to reveal to you. How does a person trust anyone?

James' family is quite wealthy, and they are generous and
loving to a fault. I pray they never find out that their daugh-
ter-in-law decided to marry their only son, with no more emotion than it would take to choose a dress for a dance.

So that I don't sound like a complete ogre (when I write it
down, it sounds appalling), I want you to know I have made
peace with all of this, and have moments of happiness, and I
believe James is happy. There were some very anxious days
on the crossing to Paris, where I was filled with the absolute
blackest thoughts about myself and everyone else. Even Paris
itself couldn't shine for me the way I had always imagined it
would, because I was crushed by the enormity of what I had
done. However, after a week of brooding and crying, which
James must have attributed to post-wedding jitters — we never
discussed it — one day, while we were in the most quaint
Parisian café sipping a strong coffee, I experienced an
epiphany of sorts.

I realized I could either go completely insane over what I
had done, which I was quickly on the verge of doing, or I
could try to love James and make a life out of the decision I
believed would save my family from ruin.

I concluded that I had chosen a path — it was my decision
— and that I could learn to be a devoted wife. I look with
renewed interest at the marriages around me, and see that
very, very few seemed fueled by passion and intimacy; rather
they seem held together by comfort and security. Now I have
little Jimmy to distract me, and fill my days with more love
than I ever thought possible.

It is so painful to write these words, not knowing if you
will ever read them. My original plan of writing you letters
detailing my feelings for you during our separation, must now

be changed, as my situation is changed. I find myself unable, though, married woman or not, to stop thinking of you. And so, I will resume this correspondence to you, my dearest, in the hopes that this simple form of communication will ease some of the suffering that is ever present in the secret regions of my heart. Whether you will ever read these words, I don't know. All I know is that my heart feels more complete now that I have resumed this small, secret connection.

My thought is that I will only write you once a year, an anniversary letter, if you will. I will tell you the things that I can tell no one else. I will tell you the things that touch my heart and soul. I have grown to love James for the good person that he is, but that is not enough to nourish my inner spirit. I crave the intellectual and emotional intimacy we once shared. That is not forgotten, nor will it ever be.

I have not written a poem this entire year, but somehow writing this letter has stirred up those old feelings inside me, and I feel, once again, after a long absence, the desire to write words on paper. To explain my heart. If such a thing can be done. Or is that like tilting at windmills?

Once more, Catherine

January 2, 1932

My dearest Sam,

Over the past year I find myself so grateful for the letters your mother writes to mine. Although our mothers are engaged in a correspondence that details only surface events ("How are you? We are fine..." and such), I still read any letters eagerly, trying to glean bits of information that might lead me to know your state of mind. Of course, it is slightly impossible to build too much on, "Sam finds the University of Arizona intellectually stimulating." I'm glad your father saw the wisdom of allowing you to go to University. You kept your end of the bargain — you worked with him on the ranch for a year, and you made the decision to further your education.

Of course, not a word from your mother about your painting. I know, though, that if you are like me (and you are), your thoughts never drift too far from the act of creation. I find myself able to go about my daily life, accomplishing all the mundane tasks that somehow fill my days, yet still, I always have a sense of poetry hovering right below the surface of my consciousness. I'm so happy to have that feeling back. The first year of my marriage I felt no sense of poetry. Having little Jimmy, and re-connecting my bond with you in this small way has given me a renewed sense of that part of me that deals with the imagination. I feel that I will have this for life. The urge to write is as familiar to me as the urge to eat or sleep. It is something that may at times in my life be dormant. But like the bulbs we plant in November that bloom in April, the words are always there, ready to burst forth with a bit of warm sunlight.

I have discovered something interesting about myself as a writer. Even though, as I mentioned, the act of creation is closely tied in with emotion, and having children is an intensely emotional experience, I feel no desire to write poetry about motherhood, or about little Jimmy. Of course, I love him dearly, and more, and his countenance is thoroughly pleasing and adorable, you would think leading to all sorts of poetic inspiration. But alas, not a single ode to babyhood has sprung forth from my heart. The poor boy...

For some reason, when I gaze upon him during those dark hours of night when no one else is up but the owls, even though my heart does little somersaults at the sight of him, I don't have the urge to "explain it" and write it down as a poem.

Thus, although I am surrounded by this vast motherly love, I am unable to put pen to paper and create. Something is lacking, some poetry essential seems to have gotten lost, I hope temporarily. Perhaps I am just tired and overwhelmed by all the changes in my life the past year. And more changes are to come — I will have another child in May.

Well, since I don't have anything too brilliant to share with you regarding my writing, I will tell you a little about my life here in Lake Forest. You would likely find it amusing and dull, and wonder that I could be satisfied with such a life, when yours is filled with study, and painting, and the great outdoors.

Mostly I am exhausted from chasing my darling baby around the house, and strolling him to town in his perambulator. You should see the fancy carriage that James' mother Emily gave us as a gift. As I stroll up Illinois Road to Deerpath, and into town, I feel as though I am pushing along a little prince, at the very least, or maybe a tiny rajah. I feel very housebound when the weather is such as it is right now, well below freezing, with damp air from the lake that penetrates your very bones. James told me for Christmas that I may have driving lessons this spring, as soon as the snow is gone, so at least I will be able to get out a bit more when the rain threatens to keep us in.

I do have a niece of Mrs. Haggarty helping me out with Jimmy, and with laundry and various other tasks. James thought she was too young, at first — she is sixteen, only four years younger than I am. But I became attached to Bridget rather quickly, and so did Jimmy. So even though she is not the most serious-minded person in the world regarding household tasks, neither am I, so I feel we are well suited. I would hate to have a stern old biddy living in my own house who would frown every time Jimmy and I came in with muddy shoes.

Now that I am a respectable matron (meaning: married

woman with a family), I am suddenly part of a complex social life that seems to have a momentum of its own. I had always sort of peripherally been aware of Mother's comings and goings socially, and I even started going with Mother to some events after I turned sixteen. But nothing really prepared me for the all-consuming whirl of meetings and luncheons that occupy the time and energies of the women of this town. Suddenly I am one of those women.

Let me give you an idea of what I mean. For example, tomorrow I am required to be at an afternoon meeting for the League of Women Voters. Mother is the chairman of the publicity committee, and I am enlisted to help her. The same evening there is a meeting of the YWCA, which is very strong here. I was a member during the better part of my girlhood. Now I am on a committee with that group to plan an upcoming fundraising dance. The next day there is a luncheon at the home of the President of the Garden Club. She is a dear friend of my mother's, and is hoping that I might join their group, a moot point that I have never planted a thing that has grown and lived; my interest in nature strictly limited to observing and writing about it. The following day I will attend a presentation and high tea sponsored by the Lake Forest chapter of the Women's Organization for National Prohibition Reform. I find that for some reason I am attracted to political issues. Maybe all those years of Father expounding on history and politics at the dinner table. Then, during the weekend there are numerous social gatherings to celebrate one thing or another, and James often requires me as a hostess at the Inn for one of the ongoing events there.

So even though my desire to write is here, hovering just below the surface of my mind and bursting to get out, my body is too busy with meetings and social engagements, and I'm not able to accomplish a thing. These other activities are accomplishments, I suppose, and I must console myself that at least I am doing something to help other people. I don't convince myself though – I know I could be doing more.

The Inn showed a profit the last two years, even during this depressed economy. James is a very good "idea" person, and he is always thinking up new ways to get local people to use the Inn, as well as promoting it to out-of-town guests. We have the weekly Kiwanis Club meetings there, as well as meetings and luncheons for nearly every other organization in town. And almost every weekend is booked with wedding receptions, birthday and anniversary celebrations, dances, fundraising events and so on. It is a little exciting, because there is always a festive atmosphere there. Even though I am not at the Inn much, occupied as I am with little Jimmy, who is now toddling about on fat, dimpled legs.

I am trying to instill a love of books in my son, even at this early age. Although he does seem more interested in gnawing on the cover of a book than looking at one. He does have one favorite that I could recite now in my sleep, and probably do. It is a charmingly illustrated book by Anne Parrish called *Floating Island*. So, my dear, the only poetry I am reading lately consists of:

> *Up the waves and over the waves and through,*
> *In spite of the swishes of tails of the fishes, we'll*
> *paddle our pod canoe!*

I don't mean to make it sound like the Depression has not hit us here in the Midwest, although the news column in the *Lake Forester* (our community newspaper) is full every week of parties, gala events, people traveling to Europe and families moving in between summer homes and winter residences. There are consistent and very real appeals from a group called the Lake Forest Community Council for jobs for the unemployed here, and also for clothing, food, and money. They say there are one hundred and sixty men and women

who are residents of Lake Forest who are unemployed and in
need of some type of assistance.

Also, there are reports of a "hobo jungle" just northwest
of Fort Sheridan, on the west side of the train tracks.
Naturally I have not seen such a thing myself, but the paper
reported just recently on a death there that sticks in my
mind. This past October, a fifty-five-year-old man died there
from alcoholism and exposure, and the authorities were trying to locate anyone who knew of possible family. Eventually
they located two sisters who came up from Ohio to claim the
body. He had been a war hero in the great war, but somehow
had become one of those faceless, nameless men one sees
these days shuffling with heads down, and eyes cast to the
pavement. As I hold dear Jimmy, I wonder (with tears in my
eyes, I confess) if some mother once held that man when he
was a babe, wanting only goodness and joy for him? What
happens to those mothers' dreams, dearest Sam?

I try not to think of dreams too often. It is difficult for
me to write this, but the dreams I had those first few months
after I returned from Sedona, seem at once so distant, and
yet as painful as if they were still newly born in my heart. I
try to not let myself think about the anguish I must have
caused you. I try not to think about the very real love I still
have for you. I try not to think about what might have happened had I left Mother and Father to sort things out on
their own, and just traveled west as I so wanted to. I wish I
could write you of these things, my dear, dear Sam, and send
the letter along to your sister Helen to give to you. Even if I
had the courage, how would it change things? For now, writing my thoughts here will have to be enough.

Perhaps it would help explain my actions if I told you
about my mother's mother. Her name was Lucinda Adams
Drake, and she traveled out here to Chicago with my grandfather Walter Drake in 1873. It took them six months to get to
Lake Forest from Massachusetts by train, stagecoach, and on

foot. One day, when my mother was eleven, her mother told her she was going to walk to a farm just south of Waukegan to get some eggs (not unheard of, apparently, back then, although I can't even imagine doing such a thing!) Grandmother Lucinda started out west on Deerpath, with a basket over her arm, neatly attired in a gray bonnet and light cloak. She was never heard from again.

To this day my mother wonders if her mother met tragedy at the hands of strangers, or if she just kept walking west. She rarely mentions it, but when she looks west, I can only imagine what she must be thinking. During our trip to Sedona that spring, I sensed Mother looking out windows and wondering. We never spoke of it. But you can see, my dear Sam, why I couldn't desert her and do the same.

Your, as ever, Catherine

P. S. Enclosed are two advertisements from the *Lake Forester*, which might give you an idea of what the Inn is like. It really is quite elegant, yet unpretentious. Lake Forest may be considered to be an enclave of society folk, but most citizens here pride themselves on being Midwestern to the core.

... ...

Every Week Day A Dollar Day
Tea Room – Today's Menu

Fresh vegetable soup or jellied consommé
Broiled whitefish – drawn butter
Broiled lamb chop – mint sauce
Roast sirloin of beef – au jus
Assorted cold meats
New potatoes in cream
Green peas
Combination salad
Hot rolls

Peach shortcake — whipped cream
Hot fudge sundae
Iced watermelon
Orange ice
Devil's food cake
Tea   coffee   milk

...   .

Imagine the following scenario: A winter with no
worries... No bills for heating or lights... No trips in
a snowstorm when there is nothing for dinner... No
problems with servants who come and go... Freedom
from those household tasks which never seem to
end... The Forest Inn offers a new winter rate for
rooms with a private bath for one or two persons—
only $85.00 per month!
Let us take the worry out of winter.
Some suites are also available for families,
also at special winter rates.

FOREST INN   LAKE FOREST

...   .

January 22, 1933

My dearest Sam,

I hardly slept at all last night. Has it really been one year
since my last letter to you? I think of you every day and
night; it seems impossible that we haven't seen one another
for three years. Have you forgiven me, dear Sam? Or will
you never be able to do so? I can still only imagine your terrible hurt upon hearing of my marriage. I believe that we
will meet again someday, although under what circumstances,
I don't know. I feel an inner peace from having met you, and

from having known a love like we knew. Many people, I suspect, never know such a joy can exist.

You surely wonder how I could have thrown such a love aside, and so abruptly. I know I can never expect you to understand how it came to pass, but you must trust me when I say I firmly believe it was the right thing for me to do at the time. And, now, looking back from the vantage point of time passed, I still feel that I made the right decision. Mother and Father are doing quite well — James and I managed to help them the first year after Father's crisis, and now financially they are doing much better. Mother has had to curtail her spending, and Father sold his car, and walks to the college, but otherwise they have been able to continue much as they always did. And they don't have me to worry about. They won't have to send me to college, or support me, because I am a married lady with someone to take care of me.

The reason I didn't sleep much last night is because I went to a very special event at Orchestra Hall in Chicago. I am putting in a clipping from the *Lake Forester* last week, which announced the event, including my very own name.

... ...

Lake Foresters to Have Boxes For Mrs. Roosevelt's Lecture

Many of the box holders for Mrs. Franklin D. Roosevelt's lecture, "Politics and Young People," on Jan. 21 at Orchestra Hall in Chicago, under the auspices of the Illinois League of Women Voters, are Lake Foresters, and include the following:

Mr. and Mrs. Silas H. Strawn, Mrs. Kersey Coates Reed, Mr. and Mrs. William O. Goodman, Mrs. Frederic W. Upham, Mr. and Mrs. Theodore W. Robinson, Mr. and Mrs. Edward H. Bennett, Mrs. Edward F. Carry, Mr. and Mrs. Robert J. Dunham, Miss Elizabeth Conkey, Mrs. Gerhardt Meyne, and Miss Harriet Stuart.
Those who are sharing boxes are Mrs. Frank P. Hixon,

*Mrs. Melvin Traylor, Mrs. J. Lawrence Houghteling, and
Mrs. Wayne Chatfield-Taylor; Mrs. Cyrus Hall McCormick,
Mrs. George H. High, Mrs. Charles S. Dewey; Mrs. Charles B.
Goodspeed, Mrs. Waller Borden, and Mrs. Kellogg Fairbank;
Mrs. James Caldwell, Mrs. Martin Smythe, Miss Bridget
Haggarty; Mrs. Chauncey B. Borland, Mrs. Albert A.
Sprague, and Mrs. Dempster; Mrs. Augustus A. Carpenter
and Mrs. Joseph M. Patterson.*

...　　...　　...

I must tell you, my dearest Sam, that this was one of the
most exciting nights of my life. I believe I told you of my
interest in politics, and of course to hear someone of Mrs.
Roosevelt's stature and intelligence was most inspiring. Just
the very presence and fact of her (very formidable, yet somehow an understanding and gentle approach) set my own mind
to going in a million different directions.

I re-read an earlier paragraph in which I state that it is a
good thing for Mother and Father to not have to worry about
me because I am a married woman, with a husband to take
care of me. How easily those words came from my mind,
flowed into my pen, and set themselves down on this paper.
Yet, when I look at them my blood runs chill. Mrs. Roosevelt
certainly isn't letting the world pass her by, playing card
games and planning committee meetings for flower shows.
She is traveling the world and making a difference in people's
lives.

How torn I am! I greatly admire that women like her can
travel the world with ease and confidence. And here I am
having just learned how to drive and navigate the bucolic
roads of Lake Forest! Last night, listening to Mrs. Roosevelt,
I felt a stirring inside me – one that I couldn't talk about to
James, or Mother or Father. In fact, Sam, you are the only
one I can think of to share this with. As close as I am to
Bridget and Margaret, we never discuss matters of the heart

or soul. Our discussions pertain solely to domestic responsibilities.

The feeling I felt was dissatisfaction. Not with my lot in life, after all, I chose that with eyes wide open; or maybe not dissatisfaction, but more of an awakening in my inner spirit. A feeling that I could do more. That I'm capable of doing more. And that perhaps I lack the courage to pursue those secret dreams I have hidden away since getting married and becoming a mother.

Of course, I am speaking indirectly of my writing. Can a woman be a wife and mother, and also be taken seriously as someone in the arts? It seems, first of all, that most writers are men, indeed, most literary writers and poets throughout time. There are women who succeed in the literary world, such as Jane Austen, George Eliot, and Emily Dickinson. But all three of them led quite unconventional lives. And Emily Dickinson is only now getting the recognition she never received during her lifetime. Then let us take modern day writers: Virginia Woolf or Katherine Mansfield, neither one leading the traditional domestic life. Both surrounded by intellectual stimulation and the constant literary conversation that comes with being in a large city with university connections.

I greatly admire Miss Harriet Monroe, the founder of *Poetry* magazine, but she never married or had a family. She followed her vision with single-minded determination, and dare I say it, selfishness. For selfishness is the one luxury you are not allowed as a wife and mother.

I must sound dreadful and if you ever do read this you will likely think me a raving and ungrateful person. But it does feel cleansing and somehow righteous to put these words on paper, even if they never do get spoken out loud.

Everyone here is reading *The Bright Land* by Margaret Fairbanks, which is a historical novel set in Galena, Illinois. It seems to me I could write a novel as good as hers, or maybe I am fooling myself. The stories are in my head, but something prevents me from making that leap and putting pen to paper with any real seriousness and discipline.

As novels go I prefer *All Passion Spent* by Victoria Sackville-West, another unconventional woman writer, and I am also enjoying the *Collected Poems* of Robert Frost, which won the Pulitzer Prize, if you will recall. I would love to write with as much ease and simplicity as Frost does. Is it easy for him, do you think, or does he have to chisel each word out of his heart, drawing blood each time?

Jimmy is the sweetest boy, and very curious. He occupies more of my time than I ever dreamed, yet I am helpless when he puts his sturdy little hand in mine and tugs at me to see some wonderful new sight, such as a leaf floating in a puddle, or a deer outside the front window. Baby Sarah is so different than Jimmy was. Where he was placid and cheerful, she is fussy and peevish. Mother says that she will most likely outgrow those traits. I hope so.

The Depression lingers on here, and it is affecting business at the Inn, yet James and his father continue to innovate and draw customers in with their ideas. The Inn is James' passion — one I don't share, but then I don't think married couples need to share the same passions and interests. We have a comfortable, pleasant life, and of course, there are Jimmy and Sarah.

What more can I say, except that during these bleak, gray January days, I look west and close my eyes, and wish the sun was warming me, and that I could see you one more time, riding your mare, and smiling down at me. Oh, dearest Sam, was it all a dream?

Yours, Catherine

P. S. You may have noticed the names in the announcement of the lecture by Mrs. Roosevelt. Mrs. Martin Smythe is

Margaret — this past year she married a naval officer who is stationed out of Great Lakes Naval Training Center. We had the reception at the Inn, of course. And Miss Bridget Haggarty is Bridget who helps me with the children and with my housework. James thought it was quite unseemly of me to take along one of the household staff to such an important event. However, he doesn't realize the close friendships women form when they spend day after day together. I see more of Bridget than I do of my own husband, like many Lake Forest women. And we are so close in age, and Bridget is so intelligent and curious, and she is very funny. When she laughs, you have to smile; you simply cannot help it. And Jimmy loves her. She was absolutely over the moon to see Mrs. Roosevelt. I think it will be the pinnacle of her life, no matter what happens to her during the next fifty years. Perhaps mine too.

Another clipping from the paper, which shows something new at the Inn:

...   .

New at the Forest Inn: Dancing to Ray O'Hara Orchestra

> *All night have the roses heard*
> *The flute, violin, bassoon;*
> *All night has the casement jessamine stirred*
> *To the dancers dancing in tune...*
> *(Alfred, Lord Tennyson)*

Enjoy our buffet dinner dances at the Forest Inn
each Thursday evening.
Dinner is served from 1 - 9 o'clock,
with dancing furnished by Ray O'Hara's Orchestra
from 7:00 - 10:30.

...   .

January 27, 1936

Dear Sam,

They are claiming that yesterday was one of the coldest days ever recorded in the history of Lake Forest. I wouldn't know firsthand, because I haven't set foot outdoors in days. It seems impossible that I will ever be truly warm again. We keep a fire going in both fireplaces, in addition to the radiator, and we all wear so many layers of clothing we look ten pounds heavier than we really are. Baby Rose looks like a plump pillow made of wool and pink baby skin!

Three years, and I talk of the weather... When, as we both know, so much has happened. I am very proud of you for completing your University degree, as your mother sent my mother the announcement. Your father, as frivolous as he once deemed a formal education to be, must respect your accomplishment and be very proud of you. But also very happy because after graduating you chose to return to the ranch. I always suspected that your ties to the ranch, to that spectacular corner of the world, were very deep, and that nothing would ever draw you away permanently. I'm sorry your oldest sister's husband died so unexpectedly, but as you've said Helen was never truly happy being away from the ranch. I remember your father jokingly remarking that if she were a man, she could have run the place at the age of twenty. Well, maybe you and she can do that together someday.

As for me, the past three years came and went like the stars in last night's winter sky. Shining bright and furiously, and then gone. Last time I wrote words to you I was rhapsodizing over the joys and wonders of motherhood with little Jimmy. Now Jimmy reads and writes and helps me with his two younger sisters, Sarah and Rose. I do cherish the lovely gifts your mother sent for each child. As I wrote to her in my thank you notes, the colorful and warm Indian blankets that she sent along for each child's birth are treasured all the more by me because their patterns and textures evoke memories of those happiest of days spent in Sedona.

Being housebound with three young children is most challenging. The winters here are so long, there are literally weeks at a time when it is impossible to set foot out of doors. I still have Bridget helping me with the children, but she no longer lives in. First of all, with the three children, we are using all the bedrooms. And also, I am happy to report last year Bridget married a very nice young man named Tim Dodd who operates a garage in town. They service automobiles, and repair damages from car accidents, and also have a car-washing service.

Bridget is expecting a baby in June, but she is still planning on coming here five days a week. She has a young niece who will help care for her own baby, so she may help me care for my children. I find it amazing how women rely on such a chain of helping and services provided by each other. For example, I have a laundress, Mrs. Nielsen, who also helps with cooking chores, but she doesn't do any of the child-care duties. She is an older woman, and my salary to her helps pay for her son to attend Northwestern University in Evanston. So, I feel a little less guilty over having a staff of two to help me run my energetic household, knowing that these women truly need the money I provide them for their much-needed services.

Mother and Father are doing very well. It is rumored that the College is building some additional homes for faculty members, so they may move into one of those homes, and rent out the house they have lived in for so long. Mother can't decide if she can bear to have strangers living in her house. Although Father points out that financially it would enable them ten years or so of "living free." Ever since the onset of the Depression, and especially after his own financial problems, Father has given new meaning to the word frugal. It drives Mother crazy. He simply refuses to buy a new shirt or suit, and instead coerces Mrs. Haggarty into sewing up things that should have been in the rag pile long ago.

Dear, dearest Sam... this is the longest I have sat with paper and pen since before I had Sarah and Rose. To think that once I dreamed my life would consist mostly of putting words on paper. And here I am, twenty-five-years old, with three young children who demand every moment of my time. I probably sound spoiled, because I do have help, but I find that caring for the children and running a household are such a complete distraction. It seems impossible, and indeed almost superfluous, to think about my dreams of writing poetry and stories. Surely, for a woman, the greatest rewards in life must be from children and family. Or so I try to convince myself.

I still continue to read a great deal. The children know that when their mother is reading a book, she is not to be disturbed unless it is something critical, like a cut finger or hurt feelings or someone needs a kiss (you see how easily I get distracted). I do find Thomas Wolfe challenging and I just finished *Tortilla Flat* by John Steinbeck. He is getting quite a bit of attention for his work. Also, I just read and found stimulating *The Use of Poetry and the Use of Criticism* by T. S. Eliot.

A most beloved literary figure in Chicago, and one of my heroines, died recently. Harriet Monroe was so persistent and brave when she began her *Poetry* magazine nearly twenty-five years ago, selling subscriptions to wealthy art patrons. I think it is one of the premier journals a poet can aspire to. Many of today's most well known poets are published there, and they are very supportive of emerging talent as well. I know it seems far-fetched right now, but I still harbor a secret dream that some day I will publish a poem in *Poetry*. And when I do, I will close my eyes for a moment, and silently thank Miss Monroe.

As for Lake Forest, we are growing and changing, but day-to-day life remains largely the same. We have a beautiful new library that brings to mind Jefferson's Monticello, and a new high school, and the *Lake Forester* now features a regular news item called "News From the Forest Inn." James is as devoted as ever to making the Inn the social hub of our busy little town. And he does succeed very well at it. He adores the children, and comes home as often as he can to make sure that I'm not too easy on them, or spoiling them, as he likes to put it. Although he is worse than I am, and can't bear for anyone to be unhappy in his presence.

As dreadful as the winters are here, summers make up for it. Every August we all have the most fun on Lake Forest Day, which has been a city tradition for many years. It's a day of carnival rides and games, and there are prizes for all sorts of fun things. It was canceled the second year of the Depression, but every year since then the city has been determined to keep it going.

There is a lovely natural beach all along Lake Michigan, and the ravines are filled with wildflowers, and there are deer and birds and raccoons wandering about our yard in better weather. Right now everything is stark and brown, but in summer it is quite lush and you fall asleep to the sound of cicadas and wake up to woodpeckers.

There continues to be a never-ending parade of luncheons, fundraisers, and meetings that keep the women in this town occupied with a fervor you can only imagine. I'm beginning to think some of the women who run these large philanthropic and social groups on the North Shore could easily give Mr. Roosevelt some stiff competition in organizational and tactical skills!

I prefer to be a worker bee, and stay in the background of most groups. Just give me a committee job, and I'll complete my small task. Although I did enjoy my involvement in the

Prohibition repeal group, especially when Prohibition was finally done away with. I actually felt that in a very small way I participated in the political process of our country. Every citizen should know the satisfaction of that feeling.

I wonder so about your life, Sam. Your mother's letters do allow me to glimpse you through a very small window. But just writing this letter to you brings back so many memories I almost can't bear to think about them. I believe that love is the most wonderful, joyous feeling in the world. But when you are separated from the person you love most in the world, love is cruel. Oh Sam, I try so hard to go about my daily life not thinking of you, and of us. My responsibilities are many and they run very deep. I have complete loyalty to James and my family. But I will always treasure what we shared in a secret part of my heart. I know that I will never have that particular form of intimacy with James. I pray that you find it with someone else, because when you know you'll never have it with the person you are wedded to for life... well, that is both hurtful and numbing.

The children's voices downstairs are reaching a fever pitch, and I imagine Bridget is ready to run out the door to her little nest in Lake Bluff, the next little town north of here. If you ever do read this, dear Sam, know how I still think of you every day with longing and love, in a part of my heart I keep for you. And that somehow writing it down here makes it real, and makes it bearable.

Yours, Catherine

June 10, 1937

Dearest Sam,

I seem to have missed January. It is always my intention

to write down my thoughts to you on January first of each year, but some years it is just too overwhelming to do so. Or what I have to say is not very interesting. For some reason I am thinking of you and Sedona today; I think it is the light. Usually the light here is solid and flat, like you are going to bump up against it. But today the sky looks as though it has no end, and the light is heavenly and lucid and colors seem bright as if someone came through with a paintbrush and painted all the trees and flowers.

I am tempted to unseal the letters in the small blue suit-case where I store them and re-read them. It would be interesting to read what I have written you over the past years. But I don't think I should do that. I might be tempted to edit, and change things. I prefer to let things fall on the page as they will. Perhaps someday we will read these letters together, or perhaps someday I will burn them. I really don't know what will become of them, or us.

I do know that I will keep writing these letters, though, because they are a lifeline to a life I once envisioned as being within my grasp. That life belonged to a young woman with dreams and ambition, and I want to remind myself, if only once a year, or every couple of years, that that woman did exist. It is so easy to forget dreams and ambition in the face of real life.

I wish I could somehow focus myself, and re-claim that part of my life that belongs to writing and poetry. My family demands seem so constant and overwhelming, that I'm not sure how to go about it. The only women writers I know of are either single, living wildly Bohemian lives, or on the brink of insanity. Do you think that to be true to your art, you have to have what is known as an artist's temperament?

My darling, the news we receive from your mother is wonderful. I am talking about your illustrations in the *Saturday Evening Post*. The story the *Post* writer did on the Grand Canyon was fascinating. How I would love to take the trip

down to the floor of that magnificent canyon. I remember
the feeling of awe I experienced when we first looked out
over the edge together. Your illustrations made the story
come alive. I got such a jolt of recognition, a visceral reaction, seeing your drawings after all these years. Seeing the
familiar lines and arcs that I grew to know almost as well as
the shape of your hands took me back in time. To our time.
Forgive my writing; my hand is shaking.

I wonder if other married women have these feelings, or
if this is just a strange quirk in my emotional makeup that is
singular to me. I love my family, and my husband provides
for us, and he is a good person and a wonderful father. But I
have never felt with James the way I felt with you, dearest
Sam. He seems content with what I give him; I am the only
person who knows that I am not giving him all I could. I
wonder if he senses how much more there is to me?

I truly thought that by devoting myself to my children
and husband these unsettled feelings would go away. But all
it took was one look at your drawings to bring back six
months that were the happiest time of my life. In one instant
I felt as bereft as a person could possibly feel from losing
what we had, and also full of an odd joy, having known that
rare love at all. I miss you, and wish you were here to hold
me. I am happy for your success, and at the same time
incredibly angry with myself because I did not follow my
heart to something that at one time was so important to me.

I recall vividly how I felt I had no choice then, and maybe
I didn't. I can't seem to shake the feeling of a parallel life
that goes on without me, a shadow life that was the life I was
meant to lead. The feeling stays with me even during times
of happiness.

The children are calling me to play on this exquisite June
day. More later.

Yours, C

(Later the same day)

It is now 10:00 p.m., and at last everyone is asleep. James is at the Inn. Tonight is the Kiwanis Club meeting, and they do tend to go on. I knew earlier that seeing your drawings had unleashed something in me, and it has taken me all day to feel settled again and figure out what that something was. Dearest Sam, I wrote my first real poem in years this afternoon while down at the beach with the children. Bridget brought her little Cathleen along with her. She has just started toddling about, and Bridget and all the children kept busy at the water's edge (the lake is still bone-chillingly cold) while I sat in the sun with my notebook.

Sam, I had such a feeling of well being when I found my old notebooks in my desk. I leafed through them and read my notes for poems, and felt a new confidence rising in me. I do have ideas, Sam, lots of them. And I must quit using motherhood and wife-hood as an excuse for not doing something that I truly feel destined for.

Perhaps the parallel life that moves along with me is not the life I would have had with you after all; perhaps it is the life I could have through my writing. That, at least, is something tangible, something I can take charge of and enter.

Yes, I have fears and insecurities about ever becoming a good enough writer. But the more biographies I read of other writers, I am beginning to think that most of them are beset by the same demons. Anyone who lives with an overactive imagination can't help but be a little crazy.

As I sat at the beach, I pieced together some of the notes I had jotted down during my time in Sedona. I came up with this little poem; not much, but it is my first attempt in years, and it felt liberating to write something at all.

Grand Canyon

The words roll off my tongue
As words of love, which we spoke

Looking out over that edge.

Kaibob, Coconino, Supai, Muav
Layers of sandstone, shale, and limestone
Laid down when the earth was smooth
Like a ball of clay, waiting to be formed.

What did Coronado think when
He first stepped toward that edge,
That ledge from which one more step
Meant a plummet through
Ages more ancient than God?

The juniper, pinon, agave, Spanish bayonet
Cling stubbornly to dizzying walls of shale
And below, the River rolls on over bleached Paleozoic
  bones
Churning, placid, roiling, joyous.

I thought for a moment I could fly into it,
Down into it, like the hawk we saw
Spiraling through rarefied air.
But then your hand steadied me
And my feet gripped the ground,
Leaving my heart under the hawk's wing.

J une 11, 1937

D ear Sam,

Two letters back to back! As I said yesterday, seeing your drawings opened something up in me. I feel as though I have been given permission (by myself) to write again. I feel such joy. I copied the poem I wrote yesterday into my notebook, and I may work on it some more, or try a new one.

But first, I have been remiss. I have talked only of missing you, and of poetry, but not a word about our lives here. I haven't been letting my brain turn completely to custard, although some days it does feel like it.

You would probably be surprised at all of the cultural opportunities that present themselves here in our little community by the lake. Chicago is only an hour away by train, but we don't have to travel to the city to get our exposure to art, music, and the literary and political world; there is something cultural happening here nearly every week. For example, last December the College sponsored Mr. Sterling North, the book editor of the *Chicago Daily News*, who presented a lecture: "Midwestern Literary Revival." His thesis was that regionalism in American literature is making progress, finally cutting into the over-touted publishing supremacy of New York City. Thanks to authors such as Willa Cather, John Steinbeck, and Erskine Caldwell, and I might add Sinclair Lewis, Carl Sandburg, and even Zane Grey, we are getting fascinating glimpses of life and cultures all over the United States.

A few weeks later our Woman's Club sponsored a very successful joint program with the PTA and the YWCA called "Roads to Peace," which was meant to arouse interest in the 12th Conference on the Cause and Cure of War (held in Chicago in January). Professor Hartzo from the College enlightened us on the very grave question of neutrality legislation, which has been of paramount concern in Congress this spring.

Also in January we had poet and critic David McCord speak on "The Poet in Print." Mr. McCord is a professor at Harvard, and he was most insightful in his observations on trends in modern poetry, obstacles faced by young poets, the influence of great poets of the past, and the part that poetry plays in our lives today. I even attended a tea for Mr. McCord, who was a weekend guest of Mrs. Francis Beidler and her son. I wanted to speak to him about women poets he might favor, but I was too nervous to speak to him in private.

I was very busy this late winter and early spring helping

out on a committee that helped with the tragedy that struck the hundreds of thousands of people living in the Ohio River Valley. You might wonder how we in Lake Forest would be involved in any way with an occurrence so far away from us. Well, the Woman's Club (we are a very active group) sponsored and staffed a booth for the collection of money, which was then sent directly every day to the Flood Relief Committee in Chicago. Our local Red Cross raised well over three thousand dollars and more than one hundred large cartons of food and clothing the first month after the calamity. Margaret's husband, a lieutenant in the Naval Reserve Air Corps, was sent to the flooded area for two months. He told us such tales of devastation; we felt we had to do something to help.

Meanwhile, at the Inn, we continue to do new things all the time. We just added a beauty salon, and we have had two well-known portrait painters staying there this spring, painting portraits of the high mucky-mucks of Lake Forest society.

I will include a clipping that will give you an idea of what our clientele are like at the Inn.

Not a high mucky-muck, Catherine

...   .

News From the Forest Inn

... Mr. and Mrs. F. E. Ogden of Clinton, Ia., were guests at the Inn during their visit in Lake Forest with their son who attends Lake Forest Academy.

... Mr. and Mrs. Lucius Teeter, Mrs. Fred Glass of Owasso, Okla., and Mrs. Jean Soutar of Sanduskey, O., were weekend guests at the Inn, as were the Misses Marian Freedman and Patricia Hawley of Geneva, and Jane Anderson of Joliet, who attended the dance at Lake Forest Academy on Saturday evening.

... Henry J. Patten has arrived at the Inn to spend the summer season there.

... Maj. and Mrs. E. W. Gaines of Fort Sheridan entertained fifty guests at a formal dinner party on Saturday evening at the Inn.

... Mrs. Della Ross Stack of Chicago has arrived at the Inn for the summer season.

... Mr. and Mrs. John E. Coleman Jr. and their daughter, Beth, arrived at the Inn yesterday to spend two weeks before moving into their new home on South Green Bay Road. Mr. and Mrs. Coleman and their daughter have been in Palm Beach for the past two months or so, and Miss Beth returned last week, and has been visiting in Chicago with her grandmother. Mr. and Mrs. Coleman motored through Virginia, and spent a few days at the Barclay in Philadelphia with their son, John III, a student at Princeton.

... Mrs. Joseph K. Toole arrives today to spend a few days at the Inn while visiting her son, Joseph P. Toole and his family of Ridge Road.

... Mrs. Arthur H. Eaton of Highland Park is a giving a bridge luncheon this noon for twelve guests at the Inn.

... Mr. and Mrs. John T. Wilson Jr. are arriving tomorrow to spend the weekend at the Inn. Mr. and Mrs. Thomas Heed, Mr. and Mrs. Martin Stevenson, and Mr. and Mrs. C. K. Foster, all of Chicago, will be weekend guests there.

... Mr. and Mrs. Winthrop Smith are moving to the Inn on Monday from the Fred Preston home on North Green Bay Road.

... Mr. and Mrs. Marvin Frost and their son Bosworth, are moving to the Inn on Monday to spend a few days before they leave for their summer home in Northeast Harbor, Maine.

... Mr. and Mrs. H. J. Briede are moving out from Chicago on Tuesday to spend the season at the Inn.

...   .

December 31, 1937

Dearest Sam,

Somehow it seems appropriate to close this year writing you a short note. I am not normally a person given to making resolutions, but I do hope that I can resolve to carry forth the work I started this past summer. Seeing your drawings inspired me, and that slight opening was all it took for me to begin a slow re-entry into my own work.

I hope you did not think it presumptuous of me to write to you and ask for one of your paintings so that I might frame it and put it above my desk. You were so kind to send one, especially the one you did send, of Canyon Creek at sunset. No doubt you were surprised to get a letter from me, as we have not corresponded openly since my marriage. And now I understand you are to be married as well.

I wish you only happiness and health in your marriage to Amanda Winslow. I vaguely remember her as "Mandy." We only met a few times, and briefly at that.

Oh, Sam, I wish that I could travel back in time, in one of Mr. Wells' time machines. Life is so strange. For one long moment everything was clear and wonderful and certain. And then, suddenly, it is years later, and nothing is as I thought it would be.

I am not unhappy, Sam. I am happy for you, and I do have a rich, full life. I wonder at times though, whether we were too careless in letting what we had slip away so easily, even though circumstances at the time seemed to dictate no other course. I know now that the feelings we shared cannot be experienced with other people just because we will it to be so. My heart does not listen to my head. But my head has determined my life so far, and I imagine it will continue to do so.

On this New Year's Eve, may your heart and head be one and find peace.

Yours, Catherine

January 1, 1938

Dear Sam,

The children are busy playing card games with James, and I am taking the rare moment of peace to go through my notebooks from last year. Yes, notebooks! I actually managed to fill three with jottings for stories, first drafts of poems, and also poems that I copied out of books written by other poets. And some reflections that I'm not sure I'll ever do anything with.

I just re-read two poems that I had copied into one of my notebooks that were written by Mrs. Howard Van Doren Shaw (Frances). She was the wife of the renowned Chicago architect who built many homes in Lake Forest, and our Market Square shopping area (he died several years ago). Frances was a lovely, energetic, talented woman who died this past October, and I feel a bit mournful reading her poems this first day of the new year, because the world will seem a lesser place without her.

The Shaw family has a wonderful home on Green Bay Road called Ragdale, which they use mostly in the summers. It was designed by Mr. Shaw to reflect the Arts and Crafts style of architecture, of which he was very fond. The entire Shaw family (there are three grown daughters) has always been devoted to the arts.

Mr. Shaw did all sorts of wonderful things at Ragdale, including building an outdoor garden theatre they called the Ragdale Ring. Frances, besides being a poet, also wrote plays, and in the summers their lucky guests would perch on folding chairs, or on limestone walls built by Mr. Shaw. The most delicate Japanese lanterns would be hung about from stone columns, casting a magical glow over both wildflowers and prairie.

Carl Sandburg, Vachel Lindsay, and Harriet Monroe have all been to plays at the Ragdale Ring over the years, and it is rumored that Miss Monroe even brought the great poet Yeats with her when he visited Chicago. I always meant to ask Frances if indeed the famous Irish poet was here, but I never did, and now I will never know for certain. Here is a simple poem I like of Frances' — she wrote it as a tribute to her husband, and to her happy times at the Ragdale Ring.

In The Theatre

Early for the play
The lights are dim,
Lonely
In the theatre he built,
Lonely, I think of him.

These walls enfold
His living thought;
Here dwells the beauty
That his hand has wrought;
In every line his heart, his brain;
Here I am near him
And he lives again.

The summer I was twelve, I developed an intense friendship with Theodora Shaw who was two grades ahead of me. We used to sit up in the apple trees and read books from the Ragdale library. When it was very hot, we would splash in the fountain her father had designed. As I recall there were three stone fish that sprayed water from their mouths and we used to pretend we were mermaids. I still remember the poem that Frances Shaw had written and inscribed at the base of the fountain. Theo and I would hold hands and chant the poem as a magical incantation against all evil: *Purling fountain cool and gray   Tinkling music in thy spray   Singing of a summer's day.*

It all seems like centuries ago. Theo and I never were close again after that summer. We both made new friends in the way girls of that age do. But every time I drive past Ragdale, even today, I can still hear the music of the fountain, the whispering flutter of Japanese lanterns in the summer breeze, and the laughter of children.

As ever, Catherine

May 26, 1938

Dearest Sam,

It is the most beautiful day of the year so far, and my thoughts turn to you. It's odd, but on certain days the elements converge in such a way that I can feel your presence beside me. If someday we do talk again, I must remember to ask you if you ever experienced the same phenomenon.

After the dull browns and grays of winter, the richness of nature in spring is almost too much to take in. It's wonderful for the children, and we go on long walks down by the lake. Jimmy is now seven years old, and is a treasure of a boy. He is thoughtful and loves to read, but has a wicked sense of humor. Sarah just turned six, and she is my challenge. She is bossy and demands a lot of attention; it is difficult to contain her — she is always spinning off on some path or another. And Rose is just like her name. At nearly three years of age, she is thoroughly pleasing to look at and be around. But without the hidden thorns.

We do get out in the winter as much as we can, although

some days in January and February you can't even step outside for more than a moment. In January there is always a
Skating Carnival at West Park, and the children participate in
races. And in February, at the Winter Club, a social and
sports club we belong to, there is an Ice Carnival as well.

Mother may have written your family about our vacation
trip last August. James and I took the children and Mother
and Father to Banff National Park in the Canadian Rockies
via the Canadian Pacific Railroad. It was magnificent country; it brought to mind the grandeur of your part of the country — even though the terrain was completely different, it was
that same feeling of nature being so overwhelmingly powerful. It was invigorating to leave the flatness of the middle
part of the country and see the different topography. The
children fell in love with the hot sulfur pools that you could
hike to right in the middle of the forest.

We may plan a trip for all of us to New York City this
summer. United Airlines has just announced a new service
from Lake Forest to New York in five hours and forty-three
minutes. You take a car to Glenview, which is a few miles
from here, board a small plane from Curtiss Air Field to
Chicago Municipal, and then on to New York. And to think
that there are people still alive who had to travel months to
get to Chicago from New York! You remember the arduous
journey I mentioned my own grandparents taking.

Recently I read *This Is My Story* by Eleanor Roosevelt, a
stunning autobiography. Also, *Last Flight* by Amelia Earhart,
which is a fascinating collection of dispatches, personal letters, diary entries, charts, and a running log of her mysterious Pacific flight last year. And most recently a new poetry
book by Edna St. Vincent Millay called *Conversations at
Midnight.*

A note about Millay: I have noticed that she is summarily
dismissed as a serious poet by some of her contemporaries,
usually male. Their criticism centers on her romanticism,

and her popularity with the general public. As if being acces-
sible to the average reader means you are writing to the bottom of the intellectual trough. I would certainly rather be
understood by one hundred average people, and touch some
sort of emotion in them, than impress one college professor
with my skillful use of language and metaphor.

Much of the so-called good poetry I read today does not
lend itself to ready interpretation. It is almost as if a group
of poets formed a secret club in which they are the only ones
who understand the secret handshake. But then along comes
someone like E. E. Cummings who reminds them that form
is there to be re-shaped and language is there to play with.

I will copy something from one of my notebooks that I
have been working on a bit — I first sketched it out during
winter (no, it does not emulate Mr. Cummings, or Miss
Millay, much as I admire their work...)

Love, C

Snow and Moon

Winter settles in, and still you are not here.
I measure days not in time
But in the hardness of the ground
The loss of leaves from trees.

At summer's end we parted
Cicadas hummed as we wept.
But already we shivered
As the air blew gray from the north.

There are two ways to feel about this
The best way is that with each season's passing
We are that much closer
To finding our way back.

The worst way is that
With every waxing and waning

Your heart will give up a piece
Of what it knows to be true.

For me there is no waning
Only waxing and waxing again
The brightness and fullness of the moon
Is infinite and frightening.

Yes, the snow will come
And I'll taste the flakes on my tongue
Not as honey from the sky
Nor as balm to soothe my heart.

Instead, I'll wonder if you, too
Are tasting winter and how it feels
As it travels down your
Throat and into your soul.

P. S. Here is a clipping from the *Lake Forester* to give you an idea of spring at the Inn:

...   .

... Baroness Frederick arrived from Chicago on Tuesday to spend several weeks at the Inn.

... Russell Tyson is arriving today from town, and will be at the Inn all summer.

... Mrs. C. M. Ely is arriving Friday to spend several months at the Inn.

... Mrs. Freeman Hinckley comes out from town on June 16 for the summer season.

... Mr. and Mrs. John Hamline Jr. are moving to the Inn on June 13 for the season.

... Mrs. William Burry Sr. will arrive in Lake Forest on June 15, and will stay at the Inn for the summer.

... William Winslow Jr. came out on Saturday to be at the Inn

for the season.

... Mrs. John Drake Jr. will move to the Inn on Tuesday for a few weeks stay.

... The Glenola Club board of Chicago is having a luncheon for twenty guests at the Inn on Wednesday.

... Out-of-town guests who will stay at the Inn for the Horse Show will include the manager, Ned King and Mrs. King, one of the judges, Henry Bell, all of New York; Dr. W. G. McQuire and family of Chicago; Mrs. M. F. McQuire and daughters of Chicago; Mrs. Wm. Miller and two daughters of Chicago; and W. J. Harris, manager of the Lexington Junior League Horse Show of Lexington, Ky.

... Lake Forest College will hold a senior dinner at the Inn for fifty guests on June 9, and an alumni breakfast for sixty guests on June 11.

...   .

January 1, 1939

Dear Sam,

No poetry news this New Year's Day. On July 6th the Inn burned to the ground. We have been immersed in the details of re-building and trying to woo back our unfortunate clientele who were at the Inn at the time. Also, all those wedding parties and gala events that were scheduled back-to-back all summer and fall... As truly disastrous as this was, amazingly no one was hurt or killed.

The fire started when a cook spilled grease on the stove. The flames were drawn by a suction fan in the kitchen up into the attic. Apparently the fire started slowly, but once it caught hold in the attic timbers it spread quickly through the east wing, into the main building and then into the west wing. The entire third floor was demolished.

We found out later that Miss Dorothy Barker, our switch-board operator, notified each of the ninety-six guests before she disconnected the switchboard and left the building.

James and his father went into action immediately follow-ing the fire, vowing to re-build a fireproof Inn, and restore its historic charm and architectural integrity. You may recall me telling you that the Inn is modeled after a historic English inn, and has an old- world charm that fits perfectly into Lake Forest.

We have had construction crews working long, hard days, and often into the evenings (thank God it has been a mild winter), and amazingly the Inn re-opened four days before Christmas. It is better than ever, and the community has been wonderful in booking holiday parties, and stopping by to compliment the staff on a job well done. Most of our origi-nal staff has returned to work, although we did hire a new woman from Evanston, Miss Anna Beth Earle to be in charge of the dining room.

You may have even seen newsreel footage of the fire. I don't know if you and Mandy ever get to a movie theatre, but we are told the that newsreel footage was shown all over the United States that first week after the fire. The manager of the Deerpath Theatre, Joseph C. Emma, took moving pic-tures of the fire when it was at its height. He sent the film to New York where Universal Newsreel developed and dubbed it, and then sent it out for distribution. One of the most wrenching experiences of my life was standing next to James in the standing-room-only showing of the newsreel here in our very own Deerpath Theatre. To watch the Inn burn like that while the commentator Graham McNamara remarked in an almost festive voice, "...See the scores of society folks driv-en from their hotel, losing their valuable belongings..." It nearly made me physically ill.

So, dear Sam... Nothing here but mind-numbing exhaustion. Between the demands of the children, and James coming and going at all hours of the night and day, I have been devoted completely to serving the needs of others. I don't mean to sound ungrateful, I truly am thankful for the health my family enjoys, and also for the fact that no one was injured or killed in the fire. But in the midst of my numbness, in the very center of my being, there is a part of me that demands nourishment. I realize now that I am the only one who can provide that nourishment. No one is going to do it for me. I must take the time to re-focus and start writing again; that always seems to help. Now, if only I can find the courage and the energy.

Devotedly, Catherine

P. S. Everyone is fine. Mother and Father are living at the college and renting out their home. After putting up a fuss, Mother has settled into her new surroundings, and is happy entertaining the college crowd. And Father is happy to be saving money. It seems like a dream to think back to that time when we almost lost everything. Now it almost seems as though the Depression, and our own financial crisis never happened. Yet at the time it was the most real thing in the world.

Bridget recently had a son, Kevin, but had such problems during childbirth her doctor told her she couldn't have more children. And Margaret and her husband had twin boys last August, and are on pins and needles over the increasing talk of the unrest in Europe affecting us here in the United States.

January 1, 1940

My dearest Sam,

When I woke this morning, the first thing I thought of was writing to you. These letters have become more than a habit; they are now a sort of mild obsession, I suppose. But somehow they answer a very real need in me to communicate with you.

Congratulations and much happiness on the birth of your son Henry. I know you will be a wonderful father, and you and Mandy must be thrilled. I wonder, dearest Sam, if you would even recognize me today. I don't feel at all like the innocent young girl who stepped off the train in Sedona eleven years ago. It certainly doesn't seem like eleven years. I still remember so much from that time; it is as clear to me as if it just happened last week.

Do you know what I miss the most? At first I missed the physical closeness we had. For years I ached from lack of your arms around me. It has never been the same with James. But as much as I miss your physical presence, I miss most dearly our conversations. Do you remember how we used to talk for hours and hours about what we were going to do with our lives, the places we wanted to see together, the paintings you would paint, and the poems I would write? You are the only person I have ever been able to talk to about my writing, and about my dreams.

James and I make plans for the future, but plans aren't the same as dreams.

I can't even say that James isn't supportive of my efforts at poetry. He is quite pleased that his wife has an intellectual side to her — he really does not like frivolous people. He enjoys it when I read a poem at the dinner table to him and the children, and he will make it a point to compliment me on whatever I have written.

The best way I can explain it is that there isn't a true *frisson* between us on an intellectual level. James may smile and nod approvingly, but he doesn't really understand why I do what I do. Why I *must* do it. He thinks that my writing is a hobby, like needlepoint, and that I only do it when bored. He doesn't know, like you sensed right away, that the desire to write, to create, is as essential and as natural to me as breathing.

Here is an example of what I mean. I read him my poem *Snow and Moon*, which I thought certainly had elements in it that might lead to a discussion, at the very least. After I read it to him, he gave a little smile and said, "That was nice," and went back to reading his newspaper. I wanted to throw something at him at him and say, "Nice! I don't want you to say it's nice. Anything but nice!" But I didn't, of course. I took my poem, went upstairs and started work on another.

I would love to sit with you and talk about Millay and Wallace Stevens and William Carlos Williams and Virginia Woolf, and about your artwork, and who is influencing you. I would love to talk with someone about things that aren't "nice," or might even be controversial, or dare I say "scandalous." Instead, I have these letters, where I can only capture a rather pathetic, one-sided attempt at that intellectual intimacy.

One of my favorite books lately is *Rebecca* by Daphne du Maurier. I love the opening line, *Last night I dreamt I went to Manderley again...* It conjures up all sorts of brooding, romantic images for me. Also, I'm stunned by *The Grapes of Wrath*, which I think deservedly won the Pulitzer. One of the reasons I love reading novels so much is that I know how difficult it is to craft a poem or short story. So I have complete and absolute respect for anyone who writes an entire book. I have no inclinations to write a novel, but I do love getting lost inside someone else's head, and taking that journey to worlds I would otherwise never know about. I think a good poem or story does the same thing though.

So much to share with you, dear Sam. Do you think we will manage to stay out of war? With Britain and France both declaring war on Germany, and Germany invading Poland, it seems somehow inevitable that we will be drawn into the conflict. I think that Mr. Roosevelt is right, though, in maintaining our neutrality as long as he can. Maybe things over there will come to a sudden cessation, and we will be spared involvement.

Here in Lake Forest everyone seems to be talking about the war in Europe. Two different families who are friends of my parents were on their annual vacations in Europe at the end of summer, and they both headed back to the U. S. on the *Normandie* much sooner than planned. Other families we know of have canceled trips to England, or have cut short their visits. A young Lake Bluff couple whose wedding I attended this past August headed for Paris, stayed there for a day, immediately went to Switzerland, and obtained passage home with some difficulty.

Our minister at the First Presbyterian Church, Dr. Oliver, was also in England this past summer, and when he returned home, he told our congregation, "There is now a calm preparedness of people ready to fight if necessary." He said that elaborate precautions are being taken for air raid defense, with provisions being stored, and trial runs being staged for air raids by the citizens.

Our Mayor Chandler asks us here to observe civic preparedness for war emergency. And our local Red Cross has put out an urgent call for all knitters and seamstresses to make clothing for war sufferers in Europe. We have sewing and knitting groups meeting a couple of days every week. I hear the click-click of knitting needles and the soft murmur of women's voices in my sleep.

Meanwhile, polo games are still played at the Onwentsia

Club, and the biggest event last summer was when George
Gershwin came to the famous outdoor theatre near here,
Ravinia. I sometimes wonder if there is a war, will it reach
us here in our little village tucked between prairie and lake?

As ever, Catherine

Here is something "not nice" that I copied out of *Poetry*
magazine last year, by E. E. Cummings:

> *love is more thicker than forget*
> *more thinner than recall*
> *more seldom than a wave is wet*
> *more frequent than to fail*
>
> *it is most mad and moonly*
> *and less it shall unbe*
> *than all the sea which only*
> *is deeper than the sea*
>
> *love is less always than to win*
> *less never than alive*
> *less bigger than the least begin*
> *less littler than forgive*
>
> *it is most sane and sunly*
> *and more it cannot die*
> *than all the sky which only*
> *is higher than the sky*

(I love the part "it is most mad and moonly." I showed it
to James and he said, "This can't be considered poetry. It
doesn't make any sense whatsoever." Help!!!)

Dearest Sam,

Well, I think I can finally say that I am developing the habit of writing every New Year's Day to report on my previous year. I don't know why, but I feel inside that we will meet again someday, and I want you to have these letters as a record of the permanence of my feelings for you. Also, by reading them, I hope you will get a sense of how I lived my life. Although at times it does indeed seem to be a dull life, hardly worth taking pen to paper over.

I should reconsider my last sentence. There are probably very few among us who lead lives of great drama. If we would keep looking only for life's dramatic moments, we would not notice the small things that add up to a life well lived. An unhurried conversation with a child on a walk through the forest. A blazing sunset that appears unexpectedly at the end of a gray, dreary day. The smell of lilacs in the air when you are walking down a sidewalk in spring. The full moon hanging heavy and white and luminescent over the lake.

Emily Dickinson rarely left her home, and would be considered to have led a most mundane life, yet she managed to infuse her writing with passion and empathy for the human condition. Yet another woman poet with an unconventional lifestyle! Are there no successful women writers who marry, have children, and lead conventional lives? I study Marianne Moore and Elizabeth Bishop and May Sarton, among some of the contemporary writers today. None married, none with children. Where does that leave me?

It's a strange dichotomy. On the one hand, I feel as though family life imbues me with the deep emotions that I need to create. At the same time, even as it does so, the sheer relentless drudgery of it threatens to destroy any spark of originality or drive.

Now that the children are getting older, I spend an inordinate amount of time driving them around to various activities. Jimmy and Sarah are both in Scouting programs, and they also spend a lot of time at the Winter Club, where there is always something going on. As a result, poor Rose, who is only five, often gets left behind, or accompanies me as I go about my appointed rounds. We stop by the Inn at least once a day, because the children love to visit James there. There are several children who live at the Inn year-round in suites with their families, and Jimmy and Sarah like to join them in terrorizing some of the stuffier guests. Also, from what I gather, there are an unlimited number of secret hiding places perfect for waging attacks against imaginary Germans and other enemy forces.

I wonder if war talk is as intense in your conversations at the ranch? Here there is talk of little else. Will we or won't we, and when... With F. D. R. in for his third term, at least we will maintain some consistency of leadership, but Margaret's husband Martin thinks that F. D. R. is too isolationist. He is certain we will be involved, and soon. I feel a little silly at times, with my knitting and sewing for the Red Cross, but they tell us that our provisions provide supplies for those in desperate need. Is it possible that if enough Midwestern mothers knit enough socks, all the children in Europe will have dry, warm feet? That is what keeps us going. One thought of our own children in such hardship, and we don't mind the hours spent knitting and purling until our hands cramp.

Maybe I should start with the beginning of the year, and work my way through. That is, if I can remember — it is always an interesting exercise to reflect on the previous year and see what sticks in your mind. In January, James and I attended the Chicago premiere of *Gone With the Wind* at the

Oriental Theatre. It was a very splashy affair, certainly the biggest and most fashionable movie opening we have ever seen here in the Midwest. We were invited by a lovely older couple who has a luxury apartment on Lakeshore Drive.

They have pots of money, inherited on both sides, and we got to know them since they spent the past few summer seasons at the Inn.

This spring a woman's clothing shop opened at the Inn. Lillian Agar is the designer/proprietress, advertising "town and country clothes." She held a wildly successful fashion show and luncheon at the Inn in April. I felt quite glamorous modeling, but came back to reality when I had to go to a PTA meeting later that afternoon.

The most wonderful event, though, was this summer. I was very proud to be part of the first Summer Writers' Conference, held in July at the Forest Inn. Rowena Bennett, who is a famous artist and writer (you may know her work, sort of folk art/primitive in bold colors), led the conference. We had speakers from the editors of *Poetry* and *Child Life*, and we had lectures and discussions by well-known poets and writers.

The last day of the conference, Mrs. Arthur Aldis, who is a much-lauded Lake Forest playwright, sponsored a poetry reading and tea at her Playhouse. I read one of my poems in front of an audience for the first time. I was in such a state all day I could barely function. But when it came time to read, I just focused on the poem, and I think it went rather well. Here is the poem I read:

Sunset on Prairie

When the day's last light falls
On the trees at the edge of the prairie
And for that moment they are bathed
With a supernatural aura,
I think of the light that comes

Just before darkness.

Already, as the tree branches glow
A black wind howls up behind me
Bringing with it bits of leaves and dirty things
A broken branch raps against the roof
Like a wild animal trying to get in.

I watch the crown of the tallest oak
As it revels in that last bit of shining glory
Before it too, gives in to
The rush of darkness
That drops over us all
Like a cloak.

(A bit dark, perhaps, but I think it sets a mood...)

Life does go on peaceably in Lake Forest, and all over the United States. But one does feel the undercurrent of the problems in Europe. It feels as though this war has always been with us. And our country is not yet even "officially" in it! So many young men are registering for the selective service, and every week two or three men from Lake Bluff and Lake Forest are called into active duty.

We all were a bit surprised when Mrs. Haggarty (you remember her; she has been a housekeeper for my mother all these years) marched to the Lake Forest post office one fall day and registered herself as an alien. It made me pause and think how many people there are living among us who are not U. S. citizens. The Alien Registration Act that was passed this summer caused rather a stampede here of domestic help, many of them fearful of registering themselves, but doing so at the urging of their employers. The idea of a government registering people in that way leaves me with an odd feeling, but I suppose it must be done under the circumstances of national security.

Here are two short little headlines from the local newspa-

per, and then a longer article that demonstrates what we are
doing with our Red Cross efforts.

... ...

News from the Forest Inn:

*... (3/28/40) Mr. and Mrs. Gene Raymond (Jeannette
MacDonald) are expected at the Inn this week.*

*... (9/26/40) Famous star of the theatre Cornelia Otis Skinner
to give benefit performance for the Lake Forest High School
Service League Scholarship Fund.*

Red Cross Needs Help
in War Emergency for Surgical Dressings

*If Lake Forest women who are bemoaning the terrifying
state of chaos existing in the world today would implement
their distress by volunteering for Red Cross work, they would
be doing something toward helping in the monumental task
confronting the Red Cross, is the assertion of the local Red
Cross work leaders. And they add, "This means you!"*

*If you will give up a few hours a week from your golf or
gardening, please report Tuesday or Thursday mornings to the
workrooms in the Lake Forest Library. You may knit or sew
or make surgical dressings. The local Red Cross work division
will have to work straight through the summer because of the
urgent need for its services. If the war were to end today, or
tomorrow, there would be a year's work to be done on behalf
of the refugees of Europe.*

*"Where We Can Help" was the title of an editorial in a
recent copy of the New York Times concerning the European
War Relief Fund. "The United States is the one country," it
says, "which because of its wealth, its resources and its geo-
graphical security, must carry the lion's share if these unfortu-
nates are to be helped. We will soon face the greatest relief
problem in the earth's history..."*

"All that we have yet given or now plan to give, publicly

and privately, is but a drop in the infinite and rising sea of human need."

...   .

Yours, as ever, Catherine

P. S. Your mother writes to my mother that so far the war effort hasn't yet directly affected operations at the ranch. She also said that an art dealer in Sedona is representing some of your paintings. I am thrilled for you. And to think I have an original painting. Will it be worth millions one day? It already is worth millions to my heart.

January 1, 1942

My dear, dear Sam,

All talk is of the war. It seems as if there was never talk of anything else. The minutest details of life seem infused with urgency and importance. Trying to think back on the year—everything centers around war efforts. Even poetry. Have you read John Ciardi's poem (it was in the July, 1940 issue of *Poetry* if you can find it, or I will copy it out for you and send it to you) called *On A Photograph of a German Soldier Dead in Poland*? I do not even try to write war poetry, because what do I really know of such things? I admire the image, *Grant him at the end his common humanity, his was the conquering step, he, the athlete.* Or *...Weight of rifle on his bruised shoulder invented manhood to him. The forward action was glory.*

Perhaps I might be able to write poems about making surgical dressings, or collecting aluminum, both of which I have spent much time at during these past months. Do you think there could be poetry in such simple acts? I don't know. Compared to the grandeur of battlefield action, I doubt whether a poem about knitting socks or collecting old cooking pans would provide much drama.

A friend of Mother's wrote us from England last spring that our Red Cross efforts seem to really be making a difference there. She writes, "A large parcel of American Red Cross clothing for evacuees has just come, and I must write to tell you the effect here. All the East End (London) and Southampton mothers and their small children have had gifts; our twin evacuees from Barmondsey have got smart blue suitings each and look really grand. It isn't only just the clothes, though they are welcome. It is the wonderful feeling that they are being sent and are successfully conveyed. If any of your friends have taken part do tell them they are appreciated and well distributed."

Mother read the letter out loud to our sewing group one Thursday morning last summer, and I must say that many heads were bent over wool and flannel, hiding tears of compassion.

Up until the attack on Pearl Harbor, the efforts here centered on the British War relief. There were at least a dozen fashion shows and as many dances and even a garden walk and flower show billed as "Gardening For Defense." Every person I know is on at least one committee, and often more than one working to raise money and goods. I've lost track of how many committees I'm involved in. Margaret and Bridget and I, along with Mother and Mrs. Haggarty often sit in my parlor, with the children playing at our feet, and knit and sew for hours. It's really not so bad. It's a very comfortable way to talk and I feel very close to these dear people. The newspaper reported that women in our local Red Cross had knitted nearly one thousand articles during the first few months of the year.

I was thrilled earlier in the year when the law was passed

releasing men over the age of twenty-eight from selective
service duty. You and James are just past that point,
although I imagine that won't stop either of you from doing
what needs to be done.

I wonder if other small towns are doing the things for the
war effort that Lake Forest is. I believe there is something
about this town that attracts successful, driven, motivated
men and women. People who thrive on challenges, and have
unlimited energy. An example is Mrs. Ruth L. Musgrave.
She has supervised, and is now the director of the construction of a recreation cottage for the service men from the
Great Lakes Naval Training Center and Fort Sheridan. The
aim is to provide a home-like atmosphere for soldiers, with
activities planned by residents of Lake Forest and Lake Bluff.
Soldiers can drop by during certain hours for a snack and a
chance to relax and read a book or magazine. We may not be
fighting in the trenches, but we are trying to do our part
here. I can't think of anyone who is not totally committed
and involved.

Mother and Father now have two young ensigns living
with them. There is an extreme shortage of rooms at the
Naval Training Center, so many families from Lake Forest
and Lake Bluff have offered extra rooms to soldiers, and are
feeding them too. I think Mother is actually enjoying the
company of these two attentive (and quite handsome) young
men.

It seems like eons ago, as everything before Pearl Harbor
does, but Mrs. Edward R. Murrow was here this fall from
London to speak about her experiences in that war-torn city.
She was here representing Bundles for Britain, and did much
to validate the feelings of all here that our hard work is necessary and vital.

This Christmas season was strange; even the children
could sense that the world has shifted somehow. We're all a
little more grateful for what we have, and more conscious

that those things we take for granted may not always be so
readily available.

Praying for peace, Catherine

P. S. Virginia Woolf's death affected me greatly. Do you
think that such talent just can't contain itself in the confines of daily life? To walk into a river with stones in
your pockets... I can't imagine what could lead you to
that point. Sometimes the idea (and the reality) of the
artistic temperament scares me. I try to suppress those
longings and yearnings, and that temperament even in
myself. I am afraid they won't fit in with my life as it is;
as I have built it.

January 1, 1943

Dear, dear Sam,

We received news of your enlistment and subsequent
assignment to the 10th Mountain Division, stationed in
Colorado. My heart goes out to Mandy. I know with two
small children, even living at the ranch with your mother and
father and sister, she must worry about your safety.

As I worry also, about your safety and James'. James also
volunteered this past year, and is currently serving with the
Quartermaster General in Washington. In a way it is difficult
to understand why men such as James and yourself would volunteer for service, when men of your age aren't being con-
scripted yet. But I suppose women will never truly understand the ways of war. Logically I understand the need to
fight this war and I believe in my heart that our country is
doing the right thing by waging an all-out effort against tyran-
ny. And if we are to believe even half the reports coming out

of Germany of atrocities being committed against the Jewish population there — then I even more firmly believe we must stay in this thing and win.

But, even knowing those things rationally and logically, in my woman's heart I cry for each and every husband, son and father who is taken from his home, and put in mortal danger. I know it sounds selfish, but I would do anything to keep the ones I love from being in this war. And at the same time I understand the absolute need.

I guess I shouldn't confine myself to discussing the war in terms of only men serving. For the first time, the list of people from Lake Forest and Lake Bluff serving in our armed forces includes several women. We actually know a young woman who enlisted, and is now somewhere in Europe. Her name is Marjorie Higgins, and she was the school nurse at the elementary school for the past four years. She is now an Army nurse, and joins other local women who are serving as WAVEs and WAACs.

We are learning to be extremely thrifty here, and to do without things that were once considered essential. To this end, Margaret, Bridget, and I are now proud graduates of Miss Ann Olson's Victory Cooking School. We look at everything with an eye to its possible usefulness for the war effort. The instruction was quite useful because we learned to adapt many recipes to the strict rationing that is in effect. It is disconcerting to be straining kitchen fats into the storage can I keep by my stove, thinking that some day that fat will be turned into nitroglycerine and gun powder. Or to think when brushing my teeth that thirty-two empty toothpaste tubes could help provide tin for a fighter plane.

I am very proud of Jimmy. The Junior Victory Army (of which he is a participant) had a school-wide salvage competition, and he collected the most tin cans, rubber, and scrap of anyone in his sixth grade class. If you can imagine, he collected six hundred and thirty-one cans! Don't even ask what our parlor looked like at the zenith of this project. I covered all the furniture in sheets, and made him stack everything as neatly as possible. But just a few weeks ago I found an empty string bean can under the sofa.

We have met so many interesting young soldiers from all over the country. Mother and Father have young men from Fort Sheridan or Great Lakes over every Sunday for dinner, and since James is gone, the children and I go over there as well. These gatherings get to be pretty rambunctious at times; very unlike the sedate dinners of my childhood, with Mother, Father, and I discussing some moment in history from Father's syllabus at the college. We are likely at dinner to be learning about tobacco growing from a Virginia farm boy, talking to a former socialite from Nob Hill, and being entertained with magic tricks by a young college student from Minnesota. I think that these young men do appreciate the break in the very serious and real work they undertake so far from their own homes. We do what we can in the hopes that somewhere else some other family will invite our own loved ones for similar dinners. These acts of kindness are what set us apart as a civilization, and this goodness must prevail.

We are still knitting, knitting, all the time knitting. I am knitting navy blue turtlenecks in my sleep, and I am also quite adept at sleeveless sweater vests. We have regularly scheduled blackout nights and air raid drills, which do bring the war home to us in a way nothing else can. I'm afraid neither the children nor I will ever be able to calmly hear the siren, without thinking of the larger implications of its scream. During those drills, I find we are all very quiet and contemplative, thinking our own private thoughts. And dearest Sam, many of my prayers are for your safety and well being. Am I selfish praying for the safety of two people I love the most (besides my children, of course), rather than concentrating on just one? I don't believe that God sets those kinds of limitations.

Poetry and war, or art and war—how do they co-exist? Can the two sensibilities even exist side-by-side, or does one naturally extinguish the other? Do you think that your view and interpretation of the world as expressed in your art will change as a result of the war? I recall thinking for the past few years that I wasn't qualified to write a poem about war, because I haven't experienced the heat of battle. Since I'm not a soldier, my feelings and thoughts about war weren't valid.

Forgive me, but since then I have changed my view on this matter. I have come to believe that women are experiencing the war as intensely as if we were indeed in a foxhole being shelled by enemy artillery. For if our loved ones are, then we are as well. The emotional bonds of a wife and mother and sister are so strong they transcend geography and time.

At any rate I decided that my war poems would try to illuminate the emotional intensity of what women are feeling on this front—the home front—as we wait and wait with breaking hearts. To that effect, here is one I am working on:

War Effort

In the pearled moonlight of a June-lit night
A ghostly garrison of pots and pans
Piled high in the empty brick fountain of Market
    Square
Await their destiny.

Bleached offerings from women who dream
That one day these carefully-hoarded scraps
Of metal will take flight and bring back
The ones they love.

In a circle where water once shimmered and sang,
This kitchen arsenal stands in silent testimony

To those who believe that wars can be won
With faith and love and yes, even frying pans.

Hopefully my attempt is somewhat better than other
rhyming efforts I have seen. I saw this dreadful ditty recently: *One drop of fat, One drop of grease, Saved and sold weekly, Will hasten peace.* Or how about, *Tin to Win,* or *Keep on
Rapping the Jap With Scrap.* These have all appeared in our
local paper.

Every night I fall into bed exhausted. Even though James
never was home that much when he was here, I realize, now
that he is gone, how much attention he showered upon the
children. I am numb from the relentlessness of being both a
mother and a father, and of course doing all I can to help
with the Red Cross and Office of Civilian Defense. I would
never complain out loud to anyone — we are all exhausted,
and some people I know have already lost loved ones. So
what is exhaustion compared to loss? I feel a kinship with
Mandy in that our thoughts are directed to you, wherever you
might be. Funny to think that she knows nothing of me (or
should I say of us?), yet I feel I share much with her.

Yours, Catherine

January 1, 1944

Dearest Sam,

Can it really be one year since I wrote you last? I am
tempted to open the letter I wrote and read what I wrote you.
It would probably sound very similar to what I will write
today.

The most chilling news we had this past year is that
Bridget's husband Tim is missing in action. She found out
on their eighth wedding anniversary. He was an army aerial

gunner, and was shot down on a flight mission over Germany on June 28.

We hear very little from James. I know he is somewhere in Europe, but his letters are brief and I am unable to read anything between the lines that might shed light as to his true condition.

Sometimes I try to imagine what it will be like when the war is over, and everyone is back home. It is nearly impossible to picture families just strolling along the streets of Lake Forest without a care in the world. Everyone now is either grim and stoic or maddeningly cheerful. But no one dares complain, because there are always those who are one million times worse off than we are. So we just pretend like these hardships are an adventure, rather like being marooned on an island, and we are awaiting rescue.

James' father is showing the strains of running the Inn without James. He does have another older gentleman, who was previously a doorman, helping him out with the management. With the labor shortage, they do what they can to keep things going. The rooms there are full all the time, because there is such a shortage of living quarters for Navy officers at Great Lakes. Also, there are many families that arrive in town to visit loved ones at Fort Sheridan or Great Lakes, only to find out that the Inn is full, and there is nowhere else to stay. Many Lake Foresters are letting rooms in their homes, either for rent, or donating them, in gratitude and compassion.

I would say that if there is one good thing I have seen come out of this war, it is that I have witnessed a truly bottomless well of human devotion and selflessness by the most ordinary of people. These are just civilians, but they engage in heroic feats of collecting money for war bonds, and organizing scrap collecting and sewing and knitting brigades, blood drives, etc. I'm sure you and James see even more intense and immediate acts of kindness and heroism. It's nearly impossible to believe that there is such terror in a world where there is also such good.

Jimmy and Sarah are in a group called "Handy Helpers." These children, ages eleven to sixteen, are pitching in to do some of the work around town that simply doesn't get done because there aren't enough men left to do it. They mowed lawns during the summer, raked leaves in the fall, and are now hiring out to shovel snow. Even Rose pitches in, and follows the group about.

I have a new talent. I am now the fastest knitter of rifle mitts in Lake Forest. Is there a sort of poetry in that? I hope so.

I do have to say, that when I am knitting or sewing or performing some mindless task, my thoughts do turn to writing. And to you. Even after fifteen years, when I think of you, and of us, it is as though everything is still fresh and new, and I am yet a yearning girl of eighteen, and you are holding me like you'll never let me go. Silly, I know, but nevertheless, my thoughts do still go there. I wonder if yours ever do, as well.

I have seen James once this past year. In August I flew to San Francisco to meet him for two days. He has always been a serious person, but now seems almost somber with worry and exhaustion. I didn't dare tell him that his father's health is poor.

My greatest pleasure in life is going to the college library once a month to read *Poetry* magazine. I often spend an entire two hours there reading just one issue, taking notes, and soaking in the intellectual stimulation.

I'm interested in a poet from California named Genevieve Taggard. I've seen several of her poems in *Poetry* over the years, and I found a copy of her *Collected Poems* in a used bookstore. I'm going to try and find out more about her. Here is a stanza of hers that I particularly like:

And even
If you are elsewhere away, and I cannot
Kiss, creating the hush,- still calm-content you:
I am child-delight of your nearness, wife and love of
your
   quickness,
Fold of your self-substance, your mingle,
Thudded where your heart is
My breath the soul of your brightness.

I must write to your mother thanking her for sending me a photo of Mandy and your two boys. Henry looks like you, and Wesley favors Amanda. How quickly life rushes by. And how little control we really have over it. You and I were once so certain that our lives would be as we dreamed that summer together, but within just a few months of that time, our lives changed irrevocably.

My Jimmy favors James as far as appearance; he is tall and thin and fair with auburn hair. He has my blue eyes, though, and I like to think he has a little bit of my way of looking at the world. There is some of the soul of a poet in him, but he has a practical, rational side to him that I imagine will rule his life. Right now, though, his life revolves around being with his friends. He has tried every sport there is, at school and at the Winter Club, and even plays golf during the summer at the public course.

Sarah is my headstrong one. She pretends to listen to me, and then does whatever she pleases. A challenge, at the very least. She is sort of severe and plain, but in a way that is almost striking. It will be interesting to see what her looks will be once she grows into them. She needs the most attention of the three children, but at the same time, she pushes you away when you try to get close. Her best trait is that she has a very strong sense of social injustice, and of what is right or wrong in a moral sense.

Rose has a head full of lavish blonde curls and her

father's brown eyes—an interesting combination. She is sweet and pleasant, and easy to get along with. Everyone remarks on Rose's easygoing nature, which I think puts Sarah even more out of sorts than usual.

My mother made a comment to me once, when I was trying to interest Sarah in a more literary book than the bland mystery stories she insists on reading over and over. Sarah was refusing my overtures (I was trying to get her to read *Anne of Green Gables*), and Mother sighed and said, "Catherine, no matter what you do, your children are going to insist on being themselves."

I think as a parent I fight that idea and embrace it as well. I wanted Sarah to read *Anne of Green Gables* because I loved it and derived so much pleasure from it. She has no interest in it however, even after I paid her a dollar to read the first chapter (I would never admit I did that to anyone else, it's so terrible!). I was so convinced that if she would just read the one chapter, she would be hooked. She put it aside after chapter one with relief and satisfaction, and never looked back. I swear she even looked at me with a glint of triumph in her eyes.

Do you ever have these clashes with your boys? Sometimes I think the entire essence of being a parent is based upon who will outwit whom.

I haven't the energy, or spirit, to write more. Unlike most women, who seem to draw such energy from dedicating themselves to the welfare of others, I find myself with dark thoughts. It is my worst character flaw. Oh, I do everything with an outward sense of cheerful duty, and I do it well. But I resent always having to put others first. I would never reveal these feelings to anyone but you, and I risk the chance that even you will think me the most selfish of women. But if I can't air my true feelings here, then I may as well never admit them even to myself... And to deny one's true feelings to oneself — well, that is as good as saying that your feelings don't have validity, just because they don't conform to everyone else's feelings.

This dilemma presents me with one of my basic conflicts as a writer. Do I go deep and put my innermost thoughts on paper, at the risk of offending others? Do I bare my soul for all of the world to see? Or do I skim the surface, with little depth charges here and there that tease the reader into thinking that I am revealing myself? And is revealing oneself the point of art? Or is it the thing that *you* see as truth and beauty — is it the small detail seen through your unique perspective that illuminates the world and holds it forth to be examined?

I imagine it must be the same with your art. We talked about this a bit when we were together, but we were so young then, and just beginning to paint and write. Indeed, I remember one conversation where we vehemently agreed that passion must rule one's art, and also one's life. Little did we know then of the practicalities that rule most lives.

Are you ever afraid that what you put down on your canvas is so personal, that you almost can't bear to have others see it, and judge it? Sometimes with my poetry and other writing I am held back by that fear. What if James reads a love poem I've written — would he ever guess that he wasn't the muse who caused its inspiration? Or would he just assume he was? Or would he even think about it as little more than a trifling piece of sweetness that his "literary" wife wrote in her spare time between committee meetings? I fear the latter.

Looking through my notebooks from the past year, I discovered this poem, inspired last summer as I sat on the edge of the prairie at Ragdale. I will copy it for you here, and you and I will be its only two readers. A pity, because I think it has some nice images, but this is one of those private ones.

Prairie Reverie

I want to crawl into the prairie grass with you,
Grasp the dirt with my hands, my knees digging in.
Grass stains on my elbows,
And the fairy dust of wildflowers sprinkled in my hair.

The joe-pye weeds will stand as sentinels
Their lavender riches offered to the sky,
And the prairie grasses, gardens of the desert,
Will move in a rhythm to match our own.

The thick air will absorb our cries
And the cries of the hawks gliding above us, watching.
Grasshoppers will alight on our shoulders
And everything will be you, the clover and the green
shafts of cutting weeds,
The yellow ragweed the color of lemons
And the slice-of-pie ghost moon in the daylight sky.

Good-bye my love, until next year...

As ever, C

January 1, 1945

Dearest,

The biggest news to report is that Bridget's husband Tim has made contact. We know he is somewhere in Germany, being held as a prisoner of war. At least, that is what we have been told by reliable sources. How these reliable sources find such things out, I can't imagine, but so far we are told to trust that he is alive.

I truly believe if it weren't for the dedication of ordinary people in these small towns like Lake Forest, the war would last even longer, and the casualties would be even worse.

Here is a clipping of a column from the local newspaper that illustrates what the ordinary person can contribute to the war effort:

...   .

... Not long ago we heard a housewife say, "Even if I did manage to save a tablespoon of waste fat every day, that would still only equal about a pound in a month's time. How could that make a difference?"

Make a difference?! My dear ladies, after that pound of waste fat is brought to the butcher, and is then sent to the war effort, it will have enough glycerin power to do any of the following things: Fire four 37 mm anti-aircraft shells, make one and one-half pounds of gunpowder, blow up a bridge and stop an invader, send a shell screaming toward the enemy, load twelve cartridges, make cellophane bags for three gas masks, provide a priceless ingredient for tannic acid salve to heal burns, or to fire ten rounds from a 50-calibre airplane cannon.

One soldier cannot win the war, but millions of fighters can. Just think what 30 million American housewives could do with all that saved waste fat. In other words, from the kitchen arsenals of America, the woman without a uniform – the housewife – could provide enough frying pan dynamite to blast the Japanese and their Axis partners into surrender. Don't underestimate! Save kitchen fats now! (P. S. Don't forget— silk stocking discards can be used for parachutes! Collect and bring to OCD HQ.) ...

...   .

It doesn't matter how much money a person has when it comes to dedication to the war effort. I bring my knitting to Red Cross meetings and am just as likely to be sitting next to a millionaire's wife from Lake Avenue, as I am Mrs. Haggarty, Bridget, or Margaret. Speaking of which, besides her twin boys, who are now six years old, Margaret now has two other children, also boys, ages three and one. And she is as happy as a mother hen.

In my letter last year I recall saying how I resent all of this work that must continually be done for others. I have been trying to improve that trait of selfishness (which I so dislike in myself) this past year, and believe I have struck a balance. I simply have no right to complain about knitting until my hands cramp, when you or James could be spending cold, rainy nights being shelled in some foxhole.

Over one thousand residents from our small community and neighboring Lake Bluff are in the armed forces. So many husbands, sons, and even daughters. The sheer number of people puts a face on the war — lots of faces. I almost hate to look at the *Lake Forester* every week, because the casualties of local boys seem to be a weekly occurrence now. I cry for every one of those boys and their families.

I am sometimes beset by the blackest moods which come at me from out of nowhere, and which I struggle to get through without letting anyone else know. I don't know exactly why these moods occur. All I know is that they have done so for the years since my marriage, and may have something to do with the abruptness of marrying James, and also with the conflicts inherent in trying to maintain a creative life when one's role to others is basically housewife and mother. Surely there must be more to me than that allotted role. There I go complaining again. See how carefully I have to keep an eye on my own actions and feelings! For really, what do I have to complain about? My children are intelligent and healthy, although Sarah constantly tests me; and my husband is a good father and provider. My parents enjoy good health, and I am fortunate to live in Lake Forest, one of the most beautiful towns in the United States, if not the world. How could I even think of myself as having problems?

The Inn is occupied these days mostly by full-time resi-

dents, although we do try to keep some of the seventy-five
rooms open for out-of-town guests. It is still the most popular
meeting spot in town for the Kiwanis Club, for the Lake
Forest Woman's Club and almost any other organization you
can think of. The dining rooms are always busy, and are
booked up for months with wedding receptions. It seems the
war has brought with it the constant pealing of wedding bells.
When a couple decides to get married, they want to do so the
next day, and have their reception at the Forest Inn that same
week. It is insanely hectic.

I can hardly imagine ever writing anything worthwhile or
original again as long as I live. I am numb with exhaustion
and worry over this endless war. Will it be like this forever?
I go through each day the same, go to bed, wake up and do it
over. I continue to write notes in my notebooks, but I fear
that when I go back to them some day after all of this is over,
I'll never know what the original inspiration was. Here are a
few random jottings: beginnings of poems, ideas that may
never go anywhere. Who knows why the subconscious mind
chooses what it does... I have learned though to write everything down that comes into my head, because if I don't, then
the thought is gone forever (maybe that wouldn't be such a
loss!). I have actually found myself going back to a one-line
phrase written five years before, and been able to feel the
spark that originated the idea, and shape a decent poem from
it. Does that happen to you with your artwork? I'll share
with you a few scribbles from my most recent notebook:

...   .

*...Last night I dreamed you were tossing snowballs at my win-
dow...*

...The sound image of bells on a Sunday morning...

*...Emily Dickinson's father rang the town fire-bell because he
wanted the citizenry of Amherst to see a beautiful sunset.
(And he was a puritanical lawyer...)*

...The image of a blind astronomer charting the constellations...

...I can wound you with my poetry, words written sharp as knives...

...The ancient oak soaked black with night and rain...

...I sleep with my poems on my bed, so that while I sleep they might fly back into my head and explain themselves...

(Untitled)

> *Midnight is the hour*
> *For interrupted dreams*
> *Waking to write poetry*
> *While all else sleep*
> *Their dreams clutched to them*
> *While I feel mine*
> *Slip away*
> *In the tricky darkness.*

Can't go on any more. Must work for a bit on some of this, maybe there is something here. I have to be like a miner and dig for the nuggets. Throw the rest back... You understand.

With love, Catherine

January 1, 1946

My dearest Sam,

One year ago it seemed as though the horrors of war would be with us forever. And now loved ones have returned home, at least for me. I feel so incredibly lucky. James is home, and Tim came back with a Purple Heart. There are more than sixty-five Purple Hearts in our two little communities of Lake Forest and Lake Bluff but then there are also forty who won't be back at all. Tim is very quiet and somber, though, where he used to be the most happy-go-lucky of men. James says the imprisonment must have affected him greatly, and it will take a while for him to adjust back to our bucolic life here. My feeling is that Bridget, Cathleen, and Kevin, and his auto business will ease him back into the world we once took so for granted.

I imagine every town in America must have their own story to tell about V-J Day. I'll never forget what I was doing at the moment peace was announced. I was peeling carrots (I can actually even smell them as I write this, the image is so strongly etched in my mind), and wishing a cool breeze would blow in from the lake. I had the radio on, and in the background I could hear the voices of the children playing in the yard. At exactly six o'clock p.m. President Truman came on the air and announced Japan's surrender.

Immediately car horns started blasting up and down our street, and I rushed out into the front yard with tears streaming down my face and yelled for the children. The four of us held each other and collapsed onto our knees on the front lawn, then we jumped up and started to dance on the grass like madmen. Neighbors all around us were doing the same. After we comforted and rejoiced with our own families, we ran to one another, neighbor or stranger, it didn't matter. It was like one hundred New Year's Eve celebrations rolled into one.

Mandy was kind enough to write to us and share the wonderful news that you arrived back at the ranch in November. I'm overwhelmed with emotion thinking about it all, and can't even put my thoughts on paper yet. It's too close still. Will write later. I promise.

Yours, Catherine

January 1, 1950

My Dear Sam,

Four years since I've written, I believe. So much has happened. Jubilation from the war's end turned to sorrow for us shortly after. I'm sorry I never responded properly to the condolences you and your entire family offered upon Jimmy's death, although James assured me he took care of all correspondence to friends and family. This is the first time I have put pen to paper since that time. I tried picking my notebooks up at different times during the past few years, but whenever I started to plumb down to the place I needed to go to write, it was just too painful.

Oddly enough, hearing this past week from your mother about Mandy's polio, I felt able for the first time to put aside my own sorrow.

First of all, you must take heart from the fact that she lived through the worst of it. Doctors now can do wonderful things with rehabilitation, and I've seen testimonials of people who have recovered fully from awful cases. And here you were probably both worried that either Wesley or Henry would get it. I know I make Sarah and Rose crazy with my worrying about them, especially during the summer months here at the lake. At home and at the Inn we follow the strictest guidelines recommended by our local hospital. But as we know, it is all mostly random chance.

I hardly know what to say that could be of any comfort to you at this time. When Jimmy died there were no words of comfort that held any meaning for me. For a long time I couldn't even bear to go near the lake that I loved so much.

As I think back on the last four years, it is with the actual sensation of being underwater. Time had a nightmarish quality to it that I imagine you are experiencing now.

It happened on a sunny day in early February, 1946. I was making Valentine cards with the girls, and Jimmy and his best friend Lee asked if they could take their sleds out. We had just had a tremendous amount of snow and a week of below-freezing weather, and the sun beckoned that day for the first time in a long while.

What happened during the next couple of hours while the girls and I were so gaily cutting out hearts and cupids, I managed to piece together from the police report and also from Lee.

The snow was just right for sledding, and the temperature had soared up to the low thirties, which compared to what we had had for weeks, was a heat wave. Lee and Jimmy pulled each other on their sleds down the streets that incline ever so slightly toward Lake Michigan. They left their sleds at the top of the bluff and slid down the ice on their bottoms to the beach. Although at that time of year you can't tell what is beach and what is frozen water.

Suddenly the "land" they were playing on broke away. It turned out they were actually on the ice, about fifty feet from the shoreline. And as that piece broke, it bumped into the ice next to it, causing it to crack as well. As Lee described on that terrible afternoon, what was once one frozen sheet of snow and ice became several blocky icebergs.

The lake underneath was choppy, and as soon as the ice floes broke free, the waves tossed the chunks of ice around like driftwood. The boys couldn't grip onto anything. As the ice floe they were on heaved in the lake, Jimmy was thrown off into the frigid water, and Lee was somehow able to fling himself onto another chunk of ice. Lee took off his jacket and tried to haul Jimmy in, but Jimmy was already too cold and numb to even hold on to the jacket. So Lee carefully but quickly jumped along the ice floes to solid ground and ran to the first house on Lake Avenue, where luckily, the housekeeper was home. The police were there in moments, but

they didn't find Jimmy until that night. It was very dangerous work for the rescue team. They had to get boats out
among the ice floes, and they themselves were in danger.
They worked with a determination I've never seen before.
Not that they thought they could save him at that point, but I
think they knew that our family couldn't bear that Jimmy was
still in that frozen water.

It has been nearly four years, and as I write about it, it is
as painful and fresh in my mind as if it had just happened
this afternoon. Jimmy would be eighteen now. When I see
his friends around town, I can't believe that they are very
nearly grown men. I guess Jimmy will always be fourteen in
my mind. How we survive losses like this and still live on, I'll
never understand. I guess, in my case, I had to go on for the
girls, and for James. But a family is never quite the same
again after something like this happens.

So, my dearest, I understand something of your loss.
Even though you still have Mandy, when the random cruelty
of life strikes at those you love, it changes you forever. Inside
you know you will never feel the same, yet externally you
have to put on a smile and get through it.

Congratulations on your first showing last summer.
Sedona is becoming quite the popular place for vacationers
from the East who want to experience a civilized and artistic
version of the West. Your mother sent my mother the postcard announcement that the gallery sent out. The painting
on the front of the postcard looks familiar somehow. Is it
meant to be the butte that you can see in the distance as you
look south from the far corral? The sky is marvelous; colors
we don't see here in Illinois. You captured the mood of twi-
light with subtlety and passion. Two difficult perceptions to
balance, but you manage to do it quite well.

Mother is talking about taking Father to Arizona next
spring. I believe she is writing to your mother to see if they
might visit the ranch. She mentioned it to me, thinking that

I might want to go with them and take Sarah and Rose along. It might do us good to get away to somewhere with wide-open spaces and an infinite sky. I remember the feeling of peace and contentment I had from the desert and mountain landscape. I truly believe that geography and geology and even vegetation affect our souls in a much greater way than we realize. Some people feel that way about the ocean. Bridget, for example. She and I and Margaret and our children went to New York City last year to see the new musical *South Pacific*. James organized the trip, saying that it was essential for my well being, and convinced Tim and Martin that I would only go if Margaret and Bridget went. We took a side trip of several days out to Long Island, and Bridget proclaimed that the very molecules of sea air were different from Illinois air, and that she felt like a re-born person walking along the ocean and listening to the waves. She is plotting to take Tim and Cathleen and Kevin to California next; she wants to compare the Atlantic and the Pacific.

I enjoyed seeing the ocean, but the desert is something altogether different. The desert air, like the prairie and lake air here, feeds my soul.

If we all come for a visit, we would want to be sure that it wouldn't be too much for Mandy. Even though I know you live in your own house, away from the main ranch, I don't know if the general excitement would be too much for her. I trust your mother will keep us informed.

A long, bleak period for poetry or imagination. When Jimmy died, I had no room in my heart or soul for poetry. Writing requires me to go into my emotional depths, and my only emotion for the past several years has been grief, something I didn't want to get any closer to than I already was. I fear I have damaged my other children and James as well, because of my own grief. It is only recently that I have allowed myself to fall back in love with Sarah and Rose. I only hope it isn't too late. Over the past four years they have turned into young women with very little guidance on my part.

The human spirit must be as resilient as prairie grass, because I never dreamed I would write poetry again, yet I'm starting to recognize the familiar urge swelling my heart, almost against its will.

As always and ever, Catherine

January 1, 1951

My dear Sam,

Perhaps these letters take the place of a journal for me. Even if you never read them, I feel I have had the advantage all these years of confiding in a best friend. A journal, written to oneself, serves a slightly different purpose. It must be like looking in a mirror. Writing a letter causes the writer to write with an eye to the reader — to that reader's sensibility. An accounting of a day, for example, would be a different accounting if I were writing it as a journal entry, than if I was writing it to you in the form of a letter.

I have debated whether or not I should bring these letters with me when we visit Sedona this June. Part of me thinks, "Of course, isn't that why you've written them — with the purpose of sharing your life and dreams with the person you once loved more than anyone in the world?" Another part of me holds back. That part of me recognizes that you may not be receptive at this time in your life to such a personal overture. That maybe you have put to rest the feelings that are still as strong in my heart as they were over twenty years ago. After all, we are both married and have families, and our lives are complicated in ways that allow no room for a passion apart from all of that.

Mother, Father, and the girls are very excited at the prospect of a train trip to the West. Even though you are as civilized in Arizona as we are here, I'm sure Sarah and Rose are expecting to see covered wagons and teepees! James, of course, will not be able to get away. He can't leave the Inn right now; his father passed away last year, and the manager ran off with one of the waitresses. With the Inn at ninety percent occupancy by residents who live there year-round, and with weekends booked up seven months in advance for weddings and banquets... Well, James has actually taken a small suite there in order to keep a closer eye on things. Ever since Jimmy died, James has involved himself even more in the business of the Inn, and of the local business community. When James is home, even after all this time, Jimmy's absence looms between us with a space as big and infinite as your Arizona night sky. James is unable or unwilling to look up into that sky, at the stars there, and is thus forced to stay in the darkness.

I have managed to ease back into my life, even though I'm afraid my relationship with Sarah is rather precarious. She is attending the University of Colorado in Boulder, and proclaims that she will never live at home again. Rose remains her own unflappable self. My long period of neglect didn't affect her the way it did Sarah. Sarah took my grieving personally, while Rose saw it more as a natural result of the accident. How two children in the same family could be so different, I'll never understand. Having been an only child, I never really thought about how siblings can be so different raised under what would appear to be the same upbringing.

Once again my life consists of committee meetings and civic responsibilities. I threw myself into these activities during the years after Jimmy's death, and now I find myself trapped. I almost resigned my membership in the Lake Forest Woman's Club, after twenty years of serving in many capacities. One of the committees I was most fond of serving on, the Literature Committee, recently took it upon themselves to visit all the businesses in Lake Bluff and Lake Forest that sell books and magazines with the purpose of checking whether or not any of the literature being sold was objectionable under the standards of the National Organization of Decent Literature. They were using a list actually provided by the U. S. government that lists reading materials considered obscene. I strongly objected to the actions of the Literature Committee, but I was in a definite minority. Perhaps they will report me to that Senator Joseph McCarthy who is using similar tactics in a more far-reaching manner.

Besides the Woman's Club, I have also remained active in the League of Women Voters. I have enjoyed that group more than the Woman's Club lately because their mission is to present issues impartially, not legislate morality. This is particularly critical during an election year. As you can well imagine Lake Forest voters, in the last election, turned out in big numbers to elect a Republican ticket. Dewey defeated Truman here by a margin of three to one.

After the war ended I was certain that no other issue or event could mobilize our small town in a similar manner. I was wrong. The polio epidemic, and the need for money and research, has spurred Lake Foresters to great heights of civic involvement. After Mandy contracted the disease, and after we started losing our own community members to the illness, I decided to work with the annual fundraising committee here. It's my way of reaching out to your family and those other families in a tangible way. And as much as I grumble and complain about my volunteer work taking up so much time and energy, I do believe deep down that it is one of the most necessary activities we as connected human beings on this planet can engage in.

Sadly, at the end of last year, Lake Forest had its first

casualty of the Korean War. It was an older brother of a friend of Jimmy's. Such a shock, once again, to see those smiling young men in their uniforms staring forth from the newspaper. At least I will never have to experience as a mother the possibility of losing a son to war. This war seems different somehow. The novelty and passion that accompanied the big war seems lacking, and instead I sense resignation and fear.

A small poem for you:

Day's Poem

I began my day
Writing a poem,
It was about something
Inconsequential
Like the view from my bedroom window
At dawn.

In between
Life
And now, writing another poem
To record
What?
Simply the passage of time?
Or the fact that I was here
I lived this day
And wrote it down.

As ever, Catherine

January 1, 1952

My dear Sam,

Carl Sandburg said when he spoke at Lake Forest College a few years ago, "Poetry is where you know how little you know and tear your hair trying to get it down on paper." I'm beginning to think I feel the same way about life, as well. At a time in my life when I thought I would certainly feel settled, I find that I am no better than an adolescent; one moment filled with euphoria at the promise of life, and the next moment taken over by the blackest of moods. In the past those moods have always entered me and then left, but lately I find it more and more difficult to shake them. The longer I live the less I seem to know and understand of life. But, like Sandburg, I try to get it down on paper.

This is a difficult letter to write. Seeing you last March meant both joy and despair for me. As soon as I saw you, all the years vanished, and I was once again a young girl stepping off a train. And you were the handsome, smiling son of my mother's best friend. It hardly seemed that nearly a quarter of a century had passed between seeing one another.

I was afraid that seeing you would be incredibly difficult. That when faced with the hard facts that we are both married, and we both have lives we just can't step out of, that my life would seem sad and futile.

Which is not how I felt at all.

I guess I am not a very modern woman, although I do pride myself on having carved out a small niche in life that is just mine, which is more than I can say most women, especially mothers, do. I surprised myself by seeing how truly conventional I am. Because even though I think of you as the great passion of my life (well, you and my writing, of course...), I still am conventional enough to recognize that I could never do anything to jeopardize my family life. Even though many of today's films seem to feature illicit love affairs and adulterous liaisons as something that everyone engages in, I know I could never betray the trust and respect of those who love me and depend on me most. And interestingly enough, you are built the same way.

It is ironic, isn't it?

Somehow it is enough for me to know that what we had once was real and lovely and true and tender. And I could see in your eyes, before we even spoke of it, that you had the same emotional depth and remembrance.

Sam, oh, Sam. To write your name is to make you real. Just as saying your name out loud makes you real. Sometimes I say your name out loud when I am putting fresh sheets on the beds, or when I am planting flowers. It makes me smile inside and out to say your name.

So, feeling this way about each other, as you said last spring you still feel about me as well, what do we do with all of this?

On the trip to Arizona with the children and my mother, I was as nervous as could be. I honestly had no idea what my reaction would be to being at the ranch again after all these years. Now, thinking back on last spring, it seems inevitable that things worked themselves out the way they did.

First of all, it was absolutely wonderful to be back in the high desert. You have no idea how different the landscape, the sky, and even the quality of light is from my little corner of the prairie. It did Mother a world of good to be there; she thrives in your climate, and I wish that she and Father would consider retiring there. Although I doubt they could ever leave Lake Forest.

Sarah and Rose (especially Sarah) also blossomed there. I think Sarah does better in a place where there is more inter- est to the landscape. She thrives on challenges; a mountain to be walked up and over, an endless desert that offers the promise of limitless horizons. She will leave Lake Forest and never look back.

Rose is content to build her life where she is. She is a creature of comfort and familiarity. She forms bonds with those around her that she wouldn't dream of severing; and even has a difficult time traveling. She adores the education- al aspect of travel, but is happiest when we are back under the canopy of elm trees that line Deerpath.

All of this, I suppose, is a roundabout way of saying that, much as my two daughters have seemingly distinct personalities with little in common, I have come to realize that I have two sides to me that may also never mesh. I have my passionate, adventurous side, which is the part of me that fell in love with you as a young girl; the side that dreams in images and writes them down. And I have the side of me that is more like Rose; the part that has strong roots in the soil where I was planted.

I'm glad that you have found an outlet for your passionate side in your artwork, but that you have also grown to love your work at the ranch. Your family is wonderful. I know for certain that even though we will always have an unbreakable bond, that you would never be able to walk away from Mandy and your family. Any more than I could do as my grandmother did so long ago (or so I believe), and leave everything behind and walk away in my apron (if I wore one), with an egg basket over my arm.

Regrets? Perhaps. As I write this, I am filled with longing and regret for what we might have had. When hard truth is staring me in the face in those long hours between midnight and dawn, I wonder how I could have married James, knowing how I loved you. Yet, I have had a fulfilling life in so many ways, that to look back with regret seems a folly. So I will not do so now.

So much of poetry is about loss and longing. Perhaps this is the human condition. Here is my small contribution to that theme, with apologies to Robert Frost...

Less Traveled

Each day
I walk the same path through the forest
Same path, every day.

One day
I don't know why,
I stepped off the path
With only one foot
It still wasn't too late.

But the other foot came down
Of its own will
And then my legs carried me
In deeper.

A branch scratched my arm
Drew blood
I stumbled over a tree root
I stepped in a hollow
Too hard and felt pain
It felt good.

And the things I heard
In the silence
The trees talking to each other
Telling their secrets
But when I looked to them for answers
They shook their leaves at me
And laughed.

On a more mundane note, I must tell you about my involvement in the Lake Forest Ground Observer Corps. I trained with thirty other volunteers under Colonel Waldo M. Allen, and we now work at our observation posts for shifts of two hours at a time. Since Bridget moved to southern California, and Sarah and Rose have been in college, I felt the need to involve myself in some way in the community again, and this seemed like something I could do well.

My shift on the observation post is shared every week with a woman who recently moved here from Washington, D. C. Her name is Lydia Grinnell, and she is a spinster who came here to take care of her ailing mother. Actually, I shouldn't call her a spinster. How outdated that sounds. She is only five years older than I am, and is the most intelligent woman I think I have ever been acquainted with. She was a freelance political journalist and has been all over the world, but is now "between things" as she puts it, taking care of her mother, as her mother is alone, except for Lydia. Funny how family ties are what really dictate most of our lives. She doesn't seem upset at leaving journalism, though. She said she has always wanted to paint, and that perhaps she will take a class to get her started.

Even though we have only worked together for a few months, I feel a strong friendship forming with Lydia. Our backgrounds couldn't be less similar, but somehow that doesn't matter; intellectually we have so much in common. I look forward to many conversational hours spent under starlit skies with her. Our shift is Sunday nights from ten o'clock p.m. until midnight.

Our observer corps is very "official," and I feel as though I'm doing my part to protect a way of life, and a country I love so much. Whether or not the threat of enemy bombings ever becomes more imminent, at least I feel that in this strange "non-war," a woman can pitch in and be of value.

Politics continues to interest me greatly, although I'm afraid that as I get older I get more rigid and opinionated, and I try hard to fight this tendency. Last year Lydia and I went to a luncheon in Evanston that featured Senator Richard M. Nixon of California, sponsored by the Women's Republican Club. Lydia didn't care for him. She forms immediate impressions of people that are usually very accurate, but to me he seemed like a typical harmless politician. With an election year coming up, I feel as though I cannot be too informed on issues and candidates, and even though I am a Democrat (much to James' dismay), I try to attend political speeches by anyone who cares to stop by this corner of the country and spout his two cents.

We had a very interesting talk right at our own Forest

Inn, when the Lions Club sponsored two servicemen back from Korea in March, who talked about their experiences there. Of course women can't attend the Lions Club meetings, but James was there and told me about it. Sadly both young men had been injured in Korea, and it brings to mind that it seems we are hardly ever far from war and its terrible effects.

While we are on the subject of war heroes, I feel I must at least mention the most exciting event to happen in Lake Forest in a while. On April 27th, General Douglas MacArthur motorcaded through Lake Forest and Lake Bluff, to the cheers of thousands of people. Mother's Garden Club was chosen to make the wreath that was placed on the War Memorial in Lake Bluff by MacArthur. You can imagine the thrill that was for her!

All in all, a wonderful year.

Yours, C

January 1, 1953

Dear Sam,

During this past year I often wondered if I would continue this one-sided correspondence. After all, if anyone knew I was writing letters to someone without ever mailing them, or for that matter, not even knowing if the addressee was ever going to read them... Well, that might be construed as being more than a little strange.

The reason I have thought about it so much, of course, is that after seeing you and realizing that neither of us was the type of person to run off and leave our families, or to carry on a clandestine long-distance love affair, I had to wonder: what kind of relationship are we left with? Of course our families will always be linked by a deep and abiding friend-

ship. And now that my Sarah will be spending her summer
at the ranch after graduating from the University of
Colorado, we will continue those links through the next generation. There couldn't be a better place for her. She is so
headstrong and unpredictable that I hope the open space will
give her room to grow into the person she so desperately
needs to become. Even though she has no idea who that person might be yet.

Rose is doing well in her second year at Lake Forest
College. She is content to live at home, and I am grateful for
her company. Surely the true test of a marriage comes when
there are no children left at home to occupy your conversations and energy, and you and your spouse are left to look at
one another across the kitchen table wondering what on
earth you're going to talk about for the next thirty years.

Things are not that bad yet; although I do secretly wonder
how James and I will manage to forge some kind of intimacy
that will allow us to have at the very least a comfortable relationship. We never talk of such things, and I suspect never
will. Another observation I have on marriage: whatever
becomes a habit in the beginning of a marriage becomes a
habit for the lifetime of a marriage. In my case, we never
had a great deal of intimate communication from the start,
and now it is a pattern that has established itself as insur-
mountably as a wall. I can actually feel words formed in my
mouth that I want to say to James, but I don't speak them. I
keep them in. I see this odd lack of true compassionate
bonding between many married couples, so I do not feel
alone. And I am luckier than most, because at least I had
that intimacy once in my life, and can draw on that to nourish my soul when I need to. Some people never experience
such true intimacy during their entire lives.

Which brings me back, in a roundabout way, to the issue
of whether I will continue to write you in this one-sided fashion. And for reasons I don't really claim to understand, I

believe I will. Perhaps just as lack of communication is a habit in my marriage, these letters to you are a habit as well. They give me a chance to reflect on my life each year, which is not a bad thing to do. And they connect me in a way to a part of myself that I don't want to ever lose. A part of me that I struggle to keep alive and flourishing. A part of me that I feel selfish claiming, yet at the same time I know is essential. A part of me that I only revealed once in my life to another person, except for in my writing. And so we will go on, if only on paper.

Recently I was looking over the notes I made in one of my notebooks; notes I took when Carl Sandburg spoke here a few years ago. He said that writers should not write as though their words would be forgotten the next moment. Writers must write as though their ideas will be listened to by another generation. He said that we need more "moon-shooters"; persons who will at least strive for perfection, whether they get there or not.

Do you feel that art has the same responsibility? That you must preserve something of what we know to be true now, so that those in the future will know how it was? It is just now dawning on me that even if you don't ever read these letters, my dear, dear Sam, perhaps someone else will. Although my fervent hope is that you and I will some day end up all wrinkled and stooped on the veranda of your ranch reading these letters and laughing and crying over their persistent, if slightly lunatic voice. If I don't destroy them, and something happens to me, there is the very real chance that a yet unknown granddaughter or grandson might read these and glimpse a window into a person he or she probably thought was rather one-dimensional. The thought of that makes my fingers fly over paper, and makes my heart smile.

We are all so much more than the face we present to the world. I guess our way of showing what is behind that face is through that which we create from our soul.

Lydia and I continue with our volunteer positions in the Ground Observer Corps. Because of the situation in Korea, our Ground Corps has been put into operation around the clock. Even though we are only civilians, we were well trained by an Army Air Force officer in identifying low-flying aircraft. It does sound silly, when you think of it, that our nation's security could rest on the shoulders of housewives and chess-playing retirees.

One of our observers caused a stir last summer when he frantically called in a report that he had seen two "strange white craft" approaching swiftly in the night mist. As it was between midnight and three o'clock in the morning, and this particular observer is known to be a bit of a tippler, we are still not sure what it was he actually saw. One curmudgeonly natural scientist in our group says our friend probably saw some early low-flying geese on the way south. There have been such reports of geese being mistaken for "unidentified flying objects" by other observers in other cities, contributing to all of those flying saucer rumors. Sounds so silly to think of alien life in space, but you hear more and more about the possibility these days.

K eeping the skies safe from enemy geese,

C atherine

P. S. Finally read Hemingway's Pulitzer winner *The Old Man and the Sea*. Just goes to show you at least one old adage for writing rings true: Less is more... I found it to be spartan, yet powerful and poetic in Hemingway's own inimitable style.

January 1, 1954

M y dearest S am,

A politically interesting year worldwide, as I think back. Eisenhower was inaugurated (Lydia was actually there, she continues to surprise; an old journalism chum invited her), Queen Elizabeth was crowned, the Rosenbergs were executed, and the U.S.S.R. exploded the hydrogen bomb.

All of which pales in comparison to the biggest event of all, and one which puts you and your family in a strange position with respect to our family.

We were thrilled when you and Mandy invited Sarah to the ranch last summer, and even more excited when it turned into a paying job. She is naturally attuned to the outdoors, and also to hard physical work. And I, of all people, can certainly understand how she found love under those circumstances. Life there for her must have been so romantic and adventurous compared to her upbringing here.

I am now adjusting to the idea that I will be a grandmother this May. I admit that my first reaction was shock, but I'm glad that she and Charlie got married at least, if somewhat after the fact, and that he seems to be a good person. I do remember his father Roy, your foreman, and I know I have met Charlie, but I obviously didn't realize what was developing between him and Sarah during that short spring visit we took. Apparently she couldn't wait to get back to the ranch after graduation for more reasons than we thought!

I fear that my initial comments to Sarah upon hearing the news were not well received, as she now refuses to speak to me; an old, unfortunate habit of ours. And she is right about James not taking the news well either. I only hope that by the time the baby is born we will all be over the shock, and be able to patch things up.

As you no doubt have discovered, my Sarah is a very headstrong young woman. Whereas her friends went to college to meet husbands, she went specifically to get a degree in sociology, so that she could work in a field that she would enjoy, and also one in which she could contribute to society's betterment. I distinctly remember her saying more than once that she wouldn't have children until she was in her thirties, if ever.

After our first trip to the ranch, she fell in love with western life, and in particular the Arizona Indian culture. The rest of us family members were in her opinion just ignorant little prairie dwellers who didn't give a fig about racism, expansionism, injustice, and poverty. With Sarah I find it difficult to get a word in to defend myself, but secretly I am glad she takes these things to heart, and exhorts others to do so as well. A social conscience is not an easy thing to develop in one's children; but I like to think that because of my own community and political involvement, my daughters will be similarly motivated.

In that vein, I have recently accepted a position as treasurer of our annual polio drive. Not only do I feel close to this issue because of Mandy, but in our own community just this past year several people have died from this horrible illness, including an eleven- year-old boy and a ten-month-old baby boy. The daughter of one of my neighbors contracted polio just after giving birth this year, and has partial paralysis. I know money alone can't solve all problems, but if it leads to better research opportunities, then I am devoted to doing all I can to help.

Once Sarah and I are speaking again, as I'm sure we will, I will tell her that next month I am attending a lecture about race prejudice, a subject she is so interested in. The Women's Association of the First Presbyterian Church is sponsoring Dr. Kathleen MacArthur, who will speak about "Human Rights and Race Relations." As Sarah pointed out on her last visit here, our local newspaper still advertises on the basis of race. Under domestic help, you still see "wanted, maid — white," or "white couple wanted for care taking." Sarah thinks that until we do away with such obvious prejudices, we will continue to be a society based on inequality. I'm sure you've heard all of this, and more, if you've spent any time with her.

James continues to work long hours at the Inn. He is always improving the services and trying to stay on top of trends that larger, more cosmopolitan hotels offer. For example, here in our little Midwestern burg we were pleased to play host to:

... ...

Mme de Rotz
Importer of European Specialties
Will exhibit in the
Forest Inn

... From Switzerland: St. Gall Blouses, Handkerchiefs, Place Mats of Sinamy with Swiss edgings
... Italian Swiss From Ticino: Unusual Beach Accessories, and Copper and Wrought Iron Handcraft
... From Italy: Cashmir, casual Jersey Coats, Stoles and Capes

... ...

Sounds very posh, doesn't it? James does have good instincts. The ladies of Lake Forest love these special events. Every day at the Inn sees a new and elaborate social calendar, with events for that day posted in the front lobby. It is still the most wonderful place for a wedding reception or special anniversary party. The history of the place, its architectural grandeur, and the level of service make it the best gathering spot on the North Shore. I confess I don't spend much time there, or as much time as I would if I were a truly devoted spouse, but I am proud of what my husband has accomplished. He is a businessman through and through, and is very connected to the community in a completely different way than I am.

How lucky you are that you and Mandy share duties at the ranch, and are both involved in its day-to-day operations. One mistake I believe I have made in my marriage is not being more involved in the one thing that is most important to my husband. When a husband and wife spend as much time apart as James and I have, they naturally build their own lives. We lead two parallel lives that rarely intersect. At times I am very lonely, dear Sam. Lonely for what might have been, and for what I imagine never will be.

This year I will be married for twenty-five years, more than half my life. What does it all mean? Will there be twenty-five more years of the same?

Better close before I get maudlin on you. Must press on...

Catherine

February 1, 1955

Dear Sam,

I couldn't write in January, as James took me to southern California to visit Bridget and Tim for our twenty-fifth anniversary. Cathleen is at UCLA studying to be a teacher, and is engaged to a young man who is studying law.

It was like traveling to another country, arriving in Pasadena in February, leaving the frigid depths of a Chicago winter. Tim's auto repair and car wash business has been very successful in southern California because everyone there drives constantly. They are planning to open another car wash in Santa Monica. Bridget has thrived in southern California. People in Los Angeles don't care about where you came from; I don't think I met a single person the whole time I was there who was a native Californian!

Bridget has opened a small flower shop in Pasadena, and she is very involved with the Huntington Museum and Gardens as a docent in their gardens. Everything is so green year-round, and there are stunning flowers blooming in February. James didn't like it as much as I did. He thinks the whole area is much too busy, and he thought the abundance of lush vegetation and blue skies was unnatural. It is rather a shock to the Midwestern soul, but one I found I could easily adjust to.

Bridget and I did have fun talking about the days when the children were young, and we were both barely adults ourselves. It was such a different time. I remember I had Bridget to help me with the children, and then Mrs. Nielsen and a succession of others as laundresses. Now I do have a maid come every week to clean the house, but I have so many appliances to do all the housework with, it almost seems redundant. No matter what is invented as a "labor-saving" device for housework, though, someone has to operate it and maintain it, so I truly have never noticed that much difference through the years in the amount of time it takes to do housework.

Now that Sarah and Rose are gone (Rose still lives at home, but keeps her own schedule, and is always either at school or with friends), I have converted Sarah's bedroom and sleeping porch into a study of sorts. I had some bookcases built in, and installed all of my poetry and writing books there. I found a wonderful old desk at a furniture consignment shop, and even bought a typewriter. I have put myself on a schedule of writing and studying, which I am trying to be faithful to; working every day from 8:30 in the morning until noon.

When I am writing, it is the only time I am truly in my own skin. I have so many thoughts in my head; getting them down on paper is the only way to release them. For the past several years, I didn't allow myself to take my writing seriously. There is *still* a part of me that says I'm an imposter, that what I have to say isn't as important as people who have intellectual training or academic degrees; that I'm just a middle-aged woman whose only accomplishments are raising a family and volunteering in the community. Perhaps you have never felt this way. I think men are raised with the notion that they have legitimate claim to whatever they want. Women wait to see if their husbands mind if they have a "hobby," and then they pursue it tentatively, and try not to make waves.

Just look at the different way in which you and I have approached our art, although you really can call your work art, my right to call my work art remains to be seen. You worked and studied and had no qualms about putting your work out in the marketplace. You pursued success in that area as a natural outcome of what you had accomplished. I, on the other hand, have never even sent a poem to a journal or magazine. My worst fear is that I will send a cherished poem to an editor and he will dismiss my work as that of another middle-aged housewife who fancies herself a writer. My other worst fear is that I will actually be successful, and then I would have to keep up a pretense that I actually know what I'm doing! Apparently my life hasn't prepared me for either success or failure, so I hedge my bets, and stay in my safe middle ground. I write, but keep it to myself.

It's hard to believe that you have seen my granddaughter before me. Sarah was very adamant about waiting until Julie was a year old, and then she would bring her here, rather than us traveling to the ranch. They are planning to be here in June, and James is going to ensconce them like royalty in a suite at the Inn. I think Sarah was surprised that I had so quickly converted her room into my writing space.

We had a very interesting guest for a dinner party in the

Hunt Room of the Inn in October. You have probably heard
of Heinrich Harrar, the author of *Seven Years in Tibet*. He
was the speaker at a benefit for the high school, and he capti-
vated everyone with the account of his amazing journey.

Does one have to travel to a faraway place like Tibet to
find the answers in life? Or can our journeys be taken in our
minds, by reading the work of others who have traveled those
paths for us?

From a grandmother who would be a wanderer
if she had the guts — C

P. S. Jonas Salk is a genius; perhaps all of the money raised
for polio research has done some good after all.

January 1, 1956

Dear Sam,

As you know, my Rose was married here last month. It
was wonderful of your mother to attend. And very brave of
her to come to Chicago in December. Since Father's heart
attack at the beginning of the year, Mother has been at odds.
James has a driver take her every day to the Lake Forest
Cemetery to put flowers on Father's grave, except in the
worst of blizzards; then James and I refuse to let her go. She
is awful to deal with on those days. We have her living at the
Inn, so that her meals are taken care of, and she doesn't have
any household responsibilities. Although James has found
her more than once instructing some poor maid or another
on the way to properly miter a sheet, or fold a bath towel.

The wedding was wonderful, but very hard on me emo-
tionally. I couldn't tell anyone of my sadness; I tried to keep
it inside around other people. But I kept thinking of Jimmy

and how it will be ten years this February that we lost him. He would be a grown man, perhaps with a wife of his own by now. I guess between losing my father and thinking of Jimmy, my nerves are just raw. And as joyous as Rose's wedding was, to a wonderful young man from the Philadelphia Main Line who is a senior at Lake Forest College, the preparations for that have left me with barely the strength to hold a pencil, and hardly an intelligent thought in my head.

To add to the emotional roller coaster that has been this past year, we also entertained Sarah and Charlie and Julie for two weeks this summer. As you will recall they were unable to attend my father's funeral because of Julie's strange fever and flu-like symptoms. I wonder how long it will be before we stop worrying about every child's fever turning into polio. In November I volunteered at the elementary school with Lydia, helping the school nurse administer the first polio vaccines to the second and third graders.

At any rate, Julie was a delightful baby, or I should say toddler, since she did toddle everywhere, and we had to keep a constant eye on her. Playing the doting grandmother, I bought her some Crayola crayons (which she promptly began to chew on, so we had to put those away for now), several wonderful books by Margaret Wise Brown, and a phonograph with records (her favorite is *Doggie in the Window*).

Charlie turned out to be a very amiable fellow, and handsome, and I am glad Sarah found him. She is so opinionated about certain things that if she had a husband who was the same way, I think they would be very unpleasant to be around. Her work on the reservation sounds interesting and essential, though, and I'm glad she has found an outlet for her energies.

Rose and Andrew left for their honeymoon in Hawaii shortly after the wedding. They flew to Los Angeles, visited with Cathleen and her fiancé, and then Bridget and Tim saw them off from Los Angeles Harbor on the luxury liner the

SS Lurline. I did mention that Andy's family is quite
wealthy, didn't I?

Lydia and I have given up our observation posts. I will
truly miss those weekly sessions under the stars with her,
where we solved all of the world's problems. But we will continue on a committee looking into civil defense for our community. The Soviet threat is not something to be taken for
granted, and I believe we should be prepared.

Margaret's oldest boy, Phillip, will enter the first class at
the new Air Force Academy in Colorado Springs, Colorado.
He was one of 330 chosen out of 6,000 applicants. We are all
very excited but that excitement is tinged with apprehension
because we also realize the purpose of the Academy is to
train young men to be prepared for war. Hopefully, this
"Cold War" we are in will never materialize into the horrors
we saw during the last decade.

This fall I attended an exhibit in Chicago that you would
have found very interesting — the first public exhibit of drawings and watercolors by E. E. Cummings. He also did a reading, which I enjoyed, having read his poetry for years.

My dearest Sam — this has been a very emotional year,
many endings and beginnings, and I think of you often, with
a smile in my heart and hoping that you only have beginnings and more beginnings. Endings are too painful.

Dreaming of desert sunsets and sunrises, C

P. S. The College trustees voted to endow a chair in the history department for Father. He would be very happy and
proud; the college was his life.

January 1, 1957

Dear Sam,

Since Mother passed away this past year, I have been at
loose ends. First of all, even after Father died, Mother had
never let me go through their things. She kept saying that
she would do it when she was ready. And she was getting
increasingly difficult to deal with the last months. We had
hired a nurse to live with her at the Inn after James was led
by a maid to a guest's room, where Mother was sitting on
their bed eating some chocolates she had found on their
dresser! She was furious with James when he insisted she
was in the wrong room. In fact she didn't even seem to realize who James was! I don't know if it was nerves, or what
kind of strange disorder it was, but I imagine it must have
been a delayed reaction to the reality of Father being gone.

I'm sorry your mother couldn't come to the funeral, but
as she is eighty-one years old, travel is now out of the question for her. I feel like I am in this strange middle area of
life. I spent the first part of my adult life taking care of my
children, and as soon as they were off on their own, my parents needed care taking. So much of a woman's life is spent
in that role.

I continue to work every morning, even if I just sit here
with pen in hand and stare out at the snow and bare maple
branches. James walks by and asks me if I'm okay, and I dismiss him with a little wave of my hand, telling him I'm working. People don't realize how much of writing consists of
staring off into space and letting things come to you. I call it
cogitating. Now that I no longer have any immediate responsibility for children or parents, I find that I'm able to think
and absorb so much more sharply. My mind never rests; it
fills constantly with images for poems and snippets of conver-

sation for stories. Last night a full-blown character came into a dream and woke me up. I sat bolt upright and started writing about him. I knew his name and the color of his hair, and even the whiskey he drank. I wonder if this is normal. I don't really know any other writers, so I haven't been able to ask anyone. I started to tell James about it, but he looked worried that I was hearing voices so I changed the subject. Does this happen to you? Do you get an image for a painting that you have to get down, just the way it comes into your head? I think it must be the same sensation.

Suddenly the world seems to be changing so quickly; or is it that as we get older, change just naturally seems more dramatic? I have been following with interest the outspoken and charismatic political leader of the Negroes, Dr. Martin Luther King, Jr. Sarah brought him to my attention, and when I see something in the newspaper about him, I clip it out and send it to her. I think that the issue of race relations is going to become enormously important in this country. Of course the situation in the South is more intense than it is in the rest of the country, but Dr. King says that even there people will have to accept desegregation of the schools.

I just read a fascinating book by another up-and-coming political leader, John F. Kennedy, called *Profiles in Courage*. There is something about Mr. Kennedy and his views that interests me greatly. The next book I read was *Peyton Place* by Grace Metalious, and if the precept that a writer should live by is to "write what you know," I think I should rather know John F. Kennedy than Grace Metalious!

I find myself drifting through life lately, but then I start to work, and that saves me. It is very strange to live life so much in your head. The odd thing is that I am not satisfied and content to enjoy my late middle years, with children gone, and no parents to look after. Instead I find myself filled with drive and ambition and a thirst to know things. That pushes me to write — the desire to understand life and explain it to myself. When I write down a story or poem on paper, I feel as though I have released it into the world, that I have taken something and explained it the only way I know how. It may not be the best way or the right way; but it is my way, and my view of the order of things. Does that count for something? Is that really art?

Of course, I assume that writers are the only ones walking around with stories going through their heads all the time. Maybe I'm wrong; maybe everyone thinks that way, in stories. Wouldn't that be wonderful!

I have started writing a novel, and right now it is threading its way through my notebooks. You are the only person I have told this to. I'm afraid if I tell anyone else that I'm writing a novel they will pat me on the head and say, "That's nice," and ask what is for dinner, or what time the next committee meeting is.

It has taken me all of my adult years to reach this point. The point where I can allow myself to do this. The story has been percolating (or cogitating) in my head for some time, and I try to dismiss it, but it always seeps back in. The main character (I think I will call her, or rather she calls herself Claire) is very persistent in her clamoring to be let out of my head and onto paper. I'm not sure if this is how other writers do it, but it seems to be the way I must do it.

Must go right now, because Claire is calling to me. Is this lunacy or is this art?

Perhaps it is both... C

January 1, 1958

Dear, dear Sam,

It has been nearly thirty years since I made the trip to Arizona that changed my life and way of thinking forever.

And finally, at last, I am writing, writing, writing. Isn't it odd that one interlude in a life could count for so much, while all the supposedly important work of my life: keeping the house in order, raising children, and working in the community seems to fade into the background. I've read of other people experiencing life-changing events, usually men, though. Men are freer to go out and be adventurous. They have always been the ones to leave the home, while the woman keeps the home. Men seem to be able to leave children. Women mostly cannot. I wonder if it will always be so.

Some day in the future either you or someone else is going to read these letters and want to ask me, "If meeting and falling in love with Sam in Arizona was so momentous, how could you possibly have chosen the path you did, and married someone else?" And there would be good reason to pose such a question. Looking back through the prism of one's past history, it is easy to say, "Oh, that's where I should have done that." Or, "How could I have not foreseen how things would inevitably turn out?" When in reality, none of us knows. The more I live of life the more I believe in its randomness. As humans we try to impose order on disorder; we especially do that as artists. We have the audacity to say, "I'm going to try and explain life. I will tell you (the reader, the art lover) how it seems to me." Yes, we think. That is it. That poem or novel explains exactly how it feels to be in a war or be a mother who loses a child. That painting represents beauty and truth.

In other words, I think we do what we do because of the way things appear to us right at that moment. That's all we can do. We trust the moment. We trust our ability to cope with a mistake, should we make one. And we live our lives.

I know I am being obtuse, when I should probably be clearer than I have ever been. But the nature of the prism is that it is always changing; we can't control it. It depends on clarity, on quality of light, and how closely the person looking into the prism chooses to look.

I knew poetry once, in Arizona, with you, and having known it, it is part of my body and soul. It is there for me to draw upon when I need it, and it needs me to explain it. I can go to the well over and over again, and fill myself with the poetry others have written. In October I saw Robert Frost at Lake Forest Academy. He was there for their centennial homecoming. Just being in his presence conjured up wondrous things in my soul.

And I have discovered a new poet, who appeared recently in *Poetry* for the first time. Her name is Sylvia Plath, and she is original and daring, and I want to find out more about her. Isn't it a little strange when we find someone whose work we connect with, we feel we have entered into their life a little? More than just a brush with greatness... It is more of an honest admiration for the hard, hard work. And the desire to know how they did it, against all the odds, against the self-doubts and the sometimes crushing weight of life.

So there, my darling: this year's rambling discourse on the things that right now are filling my life.

Neither Frost nor Plath, but trying, Catherine

 January 31, 1961

Dearest Sam,

I think it has been a couple of years since I wrote you. I suppose I could open the last envelope and look at the date, but then I might be tempted to open all the envelopes, and I don't even want to start down that path. I suddenly started getting anxious not having written you, yes, that's the exact word for how I felt, anxious, because these letters seem like a connection to something greater than myself. And isn't connection what we are all searching for? I can't explain why I need this particular connection in my life any more than I can explain why my friend Lydia paints beautiful paintings and promptly puts them up in her attic. Or why another woman friend of mine takes the most stunning photographs of the prairie and lake yet dismisses her talent as "just a hobby." How many women hide their talents under the guise of humility, where the world would be better served if they demanded the respect they should have as artists?

The past few years (I really can't remember what year I last wrote, but I feel it wasn't too far back) have been uneventful in all respects, save one.

I have put together a small book of poems. It is, in fact, sitting upon my desk right now. At least my typed-up version of it. It has gone through several incarnations, handwritten on various yellow legal pads, partially typed, handwritten again, and now finally, typed, clipped together, and sitting like a wise owl or a bomb. I don't know which. By the time you read this (if indeed you ever do) you will know whether this fledgling effort of mine came to a laudable conclusion, or whether it ended up in the bottom drawer of my desk. I look at it and I think I hate it... but at the same time I love it. Or rather I love it, and everyone else will hate it. It feels good to put this down. It has all been in my head for too long. Oh, God. Do you ever feel this way about your work?

Luckily there is much to take my mind off writing, and I often take refuge in other pursuits in order to clear my mind of the voices that are demanding to be heard and written into poems and stories.

As you know I have always taken a keen interest in politics, and to my mind last year's presidential election was one of the most fascinating ever. I doubt whether there could have been two more disparate candidates, in appearance anyway, which apparently counts for more and more now that we can see them on the television.

You'll recall that I saw Richard Nixon speak at a Republican Women's Club meeting several years ago, and that at the time I wasn't overly impressed by him (or perhaps that was Lydia). I can't remember exactly why; but there was something about him even then that seemed odd. James and I attended a fundraising dinner for Nixon held in September at the Conrad Hilton in Chicago. President Eisenhower spoke, and everyone seemed very secure in Nixon's victory. James even hosted the meetings for the Nixon-Lodge campaign group at the Inn.

But when word came through town that Senator Kennedy was going to visit the area in late October, everyone who was anyone, including many Republicans, showed up in Libertyville (a couple of towns over), where Kennedy was scheduled to stop. Lydia and I went, of course, and we used her opera glasses to get a glimpse of him. We both thought he might be too handsome for a President, although that sounds silly when you think about it. What does it matter, really? It's not like he's a movie star, trying to pose as a President.

Lydia and I helped conduct a mock election at the middle school with the League of Women Voters, and the vote was Nixon: 266, Kennedy: 74. Which predicted pretty accurately the later vote of the parents in our community who cast 5,921 votes for Nixon, and 1,936 for Kennedy.

I would like to record here (as I never told anyone else) that I voted for John Kennedy. I know James would be terribly disappointed in my doing so, so I can't tell him. Not that he would ever ask me; he just assumes he knows how I vote. Do all marriages have such strange patterns of communication, or non-communication, as the case may be?

I was thrilled when Robert Frost became the first poet in United States history to participate in a presidential inauguration ceremony. I was so moved when he read *The Gift*

Outright; watching on our television, seeing his white mane blowing in the frigid January wind, standing next to youth and beauty. The common man with a gift; an elder statesman of language, ushering in the younger statesman. Giving him permission to enter the sacred domain of public trust. Somehow it seemed holy and solemn.

It does me so much good as a writer to listen to spoken poetry and other works read aloud. As you know, I have throughout my life attended many readings and lectures by well-known writers. Hearing good writing read out loud fine-tunes your own inner ear. It's so easy to hear the false sentence, the wrong word, the stilted bit of dialogue. I have written words on the page that read nicely to the eye, but when I read them aloud to myself sounded unwieldy and false. It is one of my strange writerly quirks that I read everything I write out loud. Luckily most people who are in the house with me know of this habit, and are not startled when they pass by and hear strident sentences including many "damns" issuing forth from my study.

One of the best readings I ever attended, besides Frost, of course, was in the fall of 1959, when T. S. Eliot was the poet of honor at the 5th Annual Poetry Day celebration sponsored by *Poetry* magazine. The papers said it was the greatest crowd ever assembled in Chicago to listen to poetry. When Eliot read *The Love Song of J. Alfred Prufrock*, the hairs on my arm stood up with the first word, and didn't lie down again until the last word. It was truly a thrilling moment to witness.

I also attended a lecture recently by another famous author, Aldous Huxley, who spoke at the First Presbyterian Church here in town last year on "Freedom and Education." I am lucky to have Lydia to accompany me to everything. And you, through the act of writing these letters, to remember the best parts of my life with. Lydia and I have a wonderful intellectual intimacy, and as I've gotten older, I've decided that particular intimacy is one of the most life-nurturing gifts one can have with another human being. James tried to go to readings with me at one point in our marriage, but to him it was torture to sit through them. Luckily, he has discovered gardening as a hobby and a passion, and can spend many months now outside engaged in that. I'm glad he is working less at the Inn, and has found something creative and pleasant to occupy his time.

I find it odd and fascinating that the human race can keep writing poetry and weaving stories and painting paintings, while the experts say we are on the brink of possible nuclear destruction. Our city's first backyard bomb shelter was built this past year, and the *Lake Forester* has been running articles on civil defense techniques such as "How to Survive Nuclear Attack." Does anyone else see any irony in acts of creation coexisting with the possibility of global destruction?

We can't have come through two major wars and Korea, and not have learned to live in peace, can we? I have to put my faith in the human race; that we will somehow find a way to exist without war as a method of figuring out our problems.

Meanwhile, I send my humble little book of poems out into the world, with my hopes and dreams set down on every page.

Yours, Catherine

P. S. I don't know if I ever told you, but the painting you gave me many years ago hangs above my desk, and provides me with great inspiration. All I have to do is look into it, and I am filled with all of the yearning and loss and love that I felt so long ago. I hope I managed to put all of those emotions into my small book of poems.

June 10, 1962

Dearest Sam,

It was a nice surprise to receive your congratulatory note on the publication of my book of poems. I also cherish the exquisite turquoise and silver bracelet. I know you have already received my "polite" thank you note to you and your family for the flowers. But the bracelet is so personal in nature I feel I can only acknowledge it here. Thank you for sending it to me via Lydia, along with your very sincere and moving note. She brought both over to me this morning.

Of course you realize that the publication of a chapbook is really little more than an exercise in self-publication. Nevertheless I am pleased with the way that my small book of poetry has turned out. Even though I know that I will never be of the caliber of writer as say, Virginia Woolf or Anne Morrow Lindbergh, I do feel satisfaction and pride in my work. Midwest Press was wonderful to work with, and the woman who runs the press, Elizabeth Harding, is very supportive of women writers. It didn't matter to her that I'd never been published. She gently reminds me that could be because I have never actually sent anything out. She is certain that with our press run of five-hundred copies, she will make back her investment in printing and design costs, and perhaps even see a small profit some day. Luckily she doesn't rely on the profits from her press to put food on the table. She is from a wealthy Lake Forest family with a strong background in the arts, and has the money to support her interest.

Dearest Sam, I have actually given three readings! You, of all people, know how much I love attending author readings. So I was thrilled when the Woman's Club asked me to read from my chapbook, and speak at their monthly luncheon. I thought I would breeze through it with all the confidence in the world. But when the time came for me to read, Lydia practically had to push me out to the microphone, and then had to refill my water glass the first minute after I drained it and stood holding the empty glass looking at it like it was going to explode.

I was so nervous. I looked at all those faces, and even though many of them were familiar to me (even Bridget was visiting from Los Angeles), I was like a deer caught in a car's headlights. I wondered how I could so blithely have said yes to such an undertaking, and suddenly envied Lydia's paintings hidden in the attic where they will never be judged.

Somehow, I started to read. And as I read, I could feel my confidence coming back. The familiar words that I'd lived with for so long were like a part of me, part of my memory sense. And so I was able to finish the reading without embarrassing myself too terribly.

The poem that readers ask me about most often is a poem I wrote about the loss of Jimmy. I tell them that I've always used my writing as a means of overcoming loss or facing my fears.

The first time I had to answer a question about Jimmy's poem after a reading I almost couldn't, because all the emotions I put into the poem surfaced suddenly, and I thought I wouldn't be able to say the words. It may sound silly, but I felt Jimmy's presence there with me. Not as the young boy he was when he died. But as the young man he would have become. And I was able to talk about it. I found myself explaining, to myself as well as to the group gathered there for the reading that in writing it, I gave words and shape to a mystery—a thing that there really is no explanation for—not as we can understand with our brains, anyway. The death of a child is beyond explanation; but I had to go into that place and write about it to try and find a way to live with it.

I try to do the same thing with my other stories and

poems, Sam. I have so many questions about life. The people in my stories patiently live in my head listening to my questions for a while, but eventually they clamor to come out and be heard. It's a very weird and mysterious process, I admit, and one that I don't purport to understand, but I don't know any other way.

I wonder if it must be the same with your art, or any other artistic vision. The seed of the vision is very individual; only the artist feels it in the exact way he or she knows it must be done. The most difficult part is having the confidence and discipline to take it all the way to fruition.

Now when I attend a reading for an author, I have a new respect for the single-minded devotion behind the spoken words. The doubts suffered at midnight when everyone is asleep, and you are sitting at your writing place wondering if you are going mad. The writing of entire sentences, and paragraphs, and pages over and over, trying to find the exact way to say what needs to be said. Or what you think needs to be said, realizing that no one else gives a fig that you are even up at midnight, scribbling away like a madwoman.

My little book will disappear into the mass of printed words that are published each year, and will not affect the world in any significant way. It has, however changed my life, and I've decided that is what really matters. You ultimately do this for yourself.

This past summer I had Julie here for several weeks, and we had a marvelous time. Even though she is only eight years old, we were able to work out a schedule that enabled me to work in the mornings, leaving our afternoons and evenings free to get to know one another. She shows artistic promise, I think. Or is that just a grandmother's vanity imposing itself on her progeny?

I did take Julie to a reading with me, and she was very solemn about it. She had heard of Gwendolyn Brooks of course, as Sarah is a devoted reader of her poetry. We heard her read from her work, and it was very moving. I had a disconcerting thought while I was listening to her. Of all the readings I have attended, she is the first woman Pulitzer Prize winner I have heard. Every major reading I have gone to has been for a male author or poet. An unsettling thought, because it made me sad for all the women whose stories we will never hear. I have been listening to the male version of the world for most of my life, and I have to think that the female version must be different. I felt that with Gwendolyn Brooks. As I have with Sylvia Plath, Anne Sexton, and Maxine Kumin, who are all newly published in *Poetry*, but who are offering up new and exciting work.

> *At thirty-five*
> *she'll dream she's dead*
> *or else she'll dream she's back.*
> *All day long the house sits*
> *larger than Russia*
> *gleaming like a cured hide in the sun.*
> *All day long the machine waits: rooms,*
> *stairs, carpets, furniture, people –*
> *those people who stand at the open windows like*
> *objects*
> *waiting to topple.*

That's Anne Sexton — her first appearance in *Poetry* was last month. I'd like to find out more about her. She writes some very disturbing images in her poetry, but also true and real. What is true and real to her. That seems to be the main thing — write what is true and real to yourself. You can't worry about whether it is true and real to anyone else.

As ever, Catherine

Dear Sam,

Here, then is my letter for this year, consisting of poems and bits of this and that...

Poem for the Future

I think of you at the oddest times,
When peeling potatoes, ironing,
Sweeping the floor, folding clothes
Fresh from the dryer.

Their warmth going up through
My fingers, to my shoulders
Which you once grasped and held to you
Like you'd never let go.

Bird Walk

The last bluebirds of fall are leaving,
Disguised in a flock of sparrows.

If you wait in patience and in silence, says the leader,
The birds will come to you.

While everyone looks through tree branches for
*   warblers,*
I see a hawk circling silently against the sky.
He looks at me and speaks in a silent scream.

I stand rooted to the ground,
While a bird no bigger than my hand
Flies to the top of an eighty-foot tree.

We stand as a flock ourselves, faces turned

Prayerfully toward the sun,
Hoping to see a peregrine falcon.
But it is twenty cedar waxwings
That rise as one and head south.

(Notes from notebooks: '62)

... *I sleep with my poems on my bed so that while I sleep they might fly back into my head and explain themselves.*

... *A man finds his wife's poetry on her nightstand, and realizes it cannot be written to him.*

... *There are blind fish that became blind because where they lived was so dark they didn't use their eyes. This blindness is passed on to the next generation.*

... *Anne Hopkins, wife of the Governor of Hartford, was considered insane because she wrote and neglected her housework.*

... *George Sand sat up working all night, almost every night, for fifty years. She said, "Lovers have no patience and do not know how to hide."*

... *As with painting, the writer must see rather than look. What belongs in the work, and what is better left out for the reader/viewer to imagine?*

... *When you write fiction you have to tell the truth. This may seem a dichotomy, because in fiction you are making up stories, making up characters. But the stories and characters must be based on the truth.*

... *Writing is like setting out on a journey without an itinerary. Some people aren't cut out for that sort of life.*

Love, C

January 1, 1964

Dearest Sam,

I try to write of other events of the past year, but all memories are overshadowed by the sadness of President Kennedy's death. I had the same feeling when I heard about Pearl Harbor two decades ago; the world shifted somehow on those days, and could never be the same.

In the days after the assassination almost no one here went outdoors. Nearly every business in Lake Forest was closed. Each had a sign in their window, "We are closed to observe the death of the President of the United States." In town flags lined the main streets; they snapped briskly in the clear November air, draped with the black streamers of mourning. There were hardly any cars on the roads, and the few people out walking passed each other with solemn nods and no greetings. The Christmas wreaths and ribbons already up were a reminder that life would go on. But what kind of life could it be if such events can happen?

Rose and Andrew were here for Thanksgiving, on a short leave from their Peace Corps mission in Costa Rica. No one is more amazed than me that Rose could be off in some remote village, working under comparatively primitive conditions, far away from the comfortable life she has always led. Of course Andrew is guaranteed a spot in his father's law firm in Philadelphia when their assignment is over, but you do have to admire them immensely for taking part in the program.

They arrived here on November 21st, and we were just starting to get caught up on things the following day when the shattering news came out of Dallas. If anything, the terrible event has made them more certain of their small role in carrying on the work that President Kennedy initiated.

Their assignment there included setting up a school library, and teaching English classes to the townspeople. Rose said that the first night of class 115 adults showed up, so she and Andrew had to modify their curriculum to handle the crowd. Their reception has been good so far, although it unnerves me when I read about some countries where the native populations plaster small towns with posters saying "Yankee, Go Home," and other anti-American slogans.

Rose reminded me that if I am to worry about violence, I should look to our own small towns. The younger sister of her best friend in high school was arrested in Jackson, Mississippi, in October, on World-Wide Communion Sunday of all days, for trying to attend an all white church with a Negro girl. Rose said that the Lake Forest girl was held for twenty-four hours by Jackson police without even being allowed a phone call, and then given one hour to prepare for a trial. Whereupon she was sentenced right away to a year in jail. Very disturbing coming on the heels of the riots at the University of Mississippi, and the recent arrest of Dr. Martin Luther King, Jr. in Birmingham, Alabama.

I surprised Rose by telling her that in May I had attended a lecture at Lake Forest College by Betty Friedan, author of the new bestseller *The Feminine Mystique*. Rose was even more surprised to find my signed copy on the living room coffee table. She grabbed it and disappeared for the rest of the day, coming out only for a sandwich late in the evening.

When I asked her what she thought about the book, she said, "Well, it does put into words some of the feelings I've had about waiting to start a family." (She and Andrew have been married eight years.) Then Andrew came in and hugged her, and said to her, "Just wait until we're back in Philadelphia. When you're around my sisters, they'll make it impossible for you to not start a third branch of the Whitman family."

Whereupon I felt I should stir things up even more, and

pulled out a clipping I had saved from October's *Lake Forester* asking for nominations for "Suburban Homemaker of the Year." Having just been enlightened by Betty Friedan, we actually laughed at the official judging standards, which focused on skills in preparing meals, clothing the family, housekeeping, maintaining an impeccable personal appearance, managing the household budget, and living a spiritually uplifting life. All laudable traits to aspire to we agreed, but looking at Rose's strained reaction I couldn't help think that today's young woman may demand more from life than trained domesticity.

Now that it has been two years since my small book of poems came out, I have settled back into a normal routine, writing in the mornings and walking, when weather permits, in the afternoons. Often I stop at Lydia's after my walk, and we talk while she paints. Her painting reminds me of the Impressionist school, but she has a distinctly Midwestern flair. She does it only to please herself, and rarely lets anyone see her work, although I often try to persuade her to show at one of the local art fairs. She always waves me off, and sticks the next painting in the attic.

We do laugh at that, as my poetry book just recently experienced a meteoric rise in sales in our local suburbs due to a favorable (?) review by a literary critic at Northwestern. At least my publisher, Elizabeth Harding, said the review is favorable. According to her, anything that sells a book is a good thing. However, I am not sure I liked, "A pleasant way to spend an hour on the porch in summer." I guess I will never write a bestseller like Mary McCarthy's *The Group*. But strangely I am very satisfied with the small success I have achieved. And I keep writing, concentrating now on poetry and short fiction, although I do persist in taking notes for the novel I mentioned to you once.

Betty Friedan was the only woman author I saw last year. But I did attend a lecture by Nelson Algren at the college, who gave an interesting talk on Hemingway. Algren, of course is one of Chicago's most famous authors, but I find his work too brutal and dark to my liking. He is an interesting writer, though, and a solid craftsman.

Poetry magazine had a wonderful event just the week before Kennedy was shot (will everything before and after be colored by that tragedy?). They sponsored five poets reading their work: J. V. Cunningham, Stanley Kunitz, Robert Lowell, Karl Shapiro, and Richard Wilbur. Although part of me wanted to raise my hand and ask where the lady poets were. I hear their voices in the pages of *Poetry*, but I never see their faces. I wonder if that is part of why Sylvia Plath killed herself last February. Did she not see her work as important as her husband's? Was her spirit crushed by the world somehow? Did she think of Virginia Woolf when she did it?

And in fury left him/Glowering at the coal-fire: "Come find me"– her last taunt. Those words from a poem of hers published seven years ago haunt me today.

Once I wrote you, not long ago, about the stirring image of John Kennedy and Robert Frost at Kennedy's inauguration. An image that now comforts me is that they left our world together, the same year, two great souls mingling.

Yours, as ever, Catherine

January 1, 1965

Dear Sam,

At 54 years of age I have my first paying job. I am teaching a writing class at the community center, working with six students on their creative writing. Some big-name writers argue that writing cannot be taught, but I disagree. Certainly you can't teach someone a guaranteed formula for success, but you can teach basic elements of character development, story structure, setting, plot, conflict, and theme.

I tell my students the most important thing in becoming a good writer is to read. If you read a lot you naturally become attuned to the rhythms of what makes a story work. You develop your inner ear and a sense for what is true and what is contrived. It must be similar with painting. I imagine when you start a painting you have an image in your head, perhaps of a canyon landscape, or a sunset, or a person. Maybe you start with an emotion. By studying other paintings you get a sense of how these images have been interpreted by others, not because you want to copy their style or technique, but because that frees you to unleash the vision or voice that is in your own head. You can say, "Aha, that is how Picasso or Monet or Warhol did it." Or in my case how John Updike or Iris Murdoch or Harper Lee did it. Now this is how *I* see it... I remember the first time I read an E. E. Cummings poem. I never thought words could be written in those patterns. Something in me was freed just by that knowledge. Not that I was going to write in his style, but just knowing that I *could* was enough. I thought if he can do that, then there must be no absolute rules. Rules and structure are naturally imposed on certain forms such as sonnets or villanelles. But those rules are to be played with and shaken and thrown in the air like firecrackers or confetti. Look at a portrait painted by Rembrandt, and one painted by Picasso. How different they are, but both came from the same inner place of creation and imagination.

I am concentrating almost solely on reading women writers. It's as if they hold answers that I need. My own doubts and insecurities about my work, my fear of being mediocre — those things can paralyze me. Knowing that others have had those same paralyzing thoughts about their place in the world helps me to keep going. It is an odd thing that we do, as I remind my students. We do it because there is a force within us that pushes us to do so. No one is clamoring at the door begging for another story or poem, or another painting, although in your case perhaps that is more so. The *will* to do this art is self-directed, and it is no wonder that that provides the basis for madness among so many of our ranks. So much of the world is lived inside our heads, the line gets blurred, and sometimes we look up from what we are doing and think, what is the rest of the world doing here? I just created my own.

As always, Catherine

January 1, 1966

My dear, dear Sam,

It has been a blessing for me that Sarah, Charlie, and Julie have lived at the ranch these past years. Now that my mother is dead, and I no longer have that link of communication, I rely more than I should on Sarah's letters telling of life on the ranch. She must have a sixth sense as to how important news of you and your family is to me, for she never fails to update me on some aspect of your lives. I was very happy to hear of your successful showing at the prestigious Lowell Gallery in Scottsdale. Perhaps you recall a small painting that sold to an anonymous buyer from the Midwest. That would be me. As soon as I heard of the showing, I called the gallery and asked them to send me photos of some of your work. Not that I really needed the photos, but it was an interesting exercise. You might have guessed that I would select the one of the mare in the corral kicking up her heels and looking out beyond the fence toward the sunset and freedom and limitless horizons (at least that's how I see it). Others might simply see it as a picture of a horse... James' words, I fear. Not that I am criticizing him, mind you. I actually smiled when he said it. I decided long ago that if I were to stay sane within this marriage I would have to accept certain differences in our perspectives on things, and not get upset. Does success in a long-term marriage depend on how people accept or not accept the differences in one another? I am fond of James, and I know he loves me in his way. But many years ago I gave up on the idea of romantic love with him. It may seem silly, ludicrous even, but I don't feel I would ever have that again with anyone else. Luckily I have my writing. That is my passion.

Rose and Andrew are back in Philadelphia after their Peace Corps commitment in Costa Rica, and as Andrew predicted they are starting that third branch of the Whitman family (and Caldwell family). There is one thing that the new feminists bring up that makes sense to me more now that I am a grandmother. I really can't understand why a woman gives up her name when she marries. A person's name really is his or her most basic identity. So why does a woman have to surrender her given name when she marries? No man I know would do the same. When you think about the logic of it, there really isn't any.

Before Rose went off to meet her true and inevitable fate as wife and mother, she and Andrew stopped here for a quick visit. A friend of a friend of mine told someone else about Rose and Andrew's Peace Corps experiences, and before we knew it Rose had an invitation to go on Studs Terkel's radio show, "Wax Museum." She spoke about her experiences along with other women who had been in the Peace Corps from Uganda and Tibet. I was very proud of her, and of the other women on the show as well.

I think it was our third summer with Julie here. In those summers she has changed from a child skipping rope and playing hopscotch for hours, to a pre-teen who listens to the radio day and night hoping to hear a song by the Beatles. The teen center in town hosted a Beatles Night while she was here, and that sent her into a complete swoon. She is a sweet girl though, and we continue our pattern of working together.

She likes to be near me when I work in the mornings, and she seems to innately understand that she is not to disturb my work then. In the afternoons we walk; often around the woods and prairie surrounding Ragdale, or sometimes we walk to the lake. I'll never feel the same way about the lake as I did before Jimmy died there. I used to love sitting down there for hours in the sun, reading and writing. Even though it has been so many years, I have not been able to reconcile his death with the hard fact that the lake is where he died.

Now that Julie is entering her teen years, the world seems a more dangerous place than ever before. I am much more fearful for her than I was with Sarah and Rose. The world seems poised on the brink of many changes, and not all of them will be achieved without cost.

Do we write and make art to try and make sense of the world? To impose order on chaos? To say, "Look, this is something beautiful and lasting." Indeed, what can we do that is nobler than that?

Love, as ever, C

January 1, 1968

Dearest Sam,

Unbelievably, I have been meaning to write to you since last January first. In my head I have written you every day, but somehow I never actually sat down to what is now an almost yearly ritual. I gave up on resolutions long ago, and at the age of fifty-seven, I am an unlikely candidate for self-improvement of any kind.

Where to begin, where to begin...

And, also, I wonder what you would want to know? I have always taken the liberty in this one-sided correspondence, of telling you only what I wish. Certainly I sum up the year in tangible ways such as family milestones, politics, and community events, but I suppose by the very act of choosing what I will tell you, I am editing my life as I go. The intangible things go into my poems and stories.

I continue to work and teach. I have a young woman student, Jane Kendall, who is very promising. She is quite timid and insecure about her work, but I hope with the encouragement of the class she will become more confident. As one who has harbored secret but very strong ambitions for so long, I recognize that kindred spirit in someone else.

During all these years I have been writing you, at some point in each decade our country and my very own community is affected by war. And wartime is always reflected in our art. *Poetry* magazine has featured many powerful war poems about Vietnam, just as they did when we were in the midst of World War II.

For a long time I truly believed that the conflict in Vietnam would remain just that — a conflict. But it becomes more and more obvious that this war has elements unlike past wars — instead of bringing our country together in a united front against the "enemy," it has divided neighbor against neighbor.

How sad it is to see the handsome young faces once again on the front page of the local newspaper. The tally of war dead in our little towns of Lake Forest and Lake Bluff is slowly creeping upward, and for the first time last year, Vietnam veterans marched in the Lake Forest Day parade. Seeing the different generations represented in the parade made me wonder if there will ever be a generation untouched by conflict.

I am pasting here a clipping about a recent event at the Inn:

...   .

... Last week at the Forest Inn, the Chamber of Commerce hosted Lieutenant Colonel Frank McDermott, a resident of Lake Forest, who was here on leave from his advisory position in Vietnam. He showed two short films and gave a talk about our civil and combat actions in Vietnam. He also presented a letter to the Chamber from a Mother Superior of an orphanage near Phan Thiet City. The contents of the letter are reproduced here:

Dear Lt. Col: In our abbey there are 10 nuns and 50 children aged from 13 years and older. We are now lacked everything. At many times we intended to give them back to their families. But when hearing Lt. Col, wants to help us, that's really a happiness for the children.

Dear Sir, if possible please give them as necessary as: Mosquito nets, materials or clothing, butter, milk, etc.

Dear Sir, about the quality is according to you. Respectfully yours, Loewe Pham Thi Can

...   .

So, once again our small, Midwestern community is called upon to give help to a part of the world most of us have never been to, nor will ever go to.

Sometimes, when I'm walking our quiet streets under arched elms, with cicadas shrilling and sprinklers making their lazy, hypnotic circles, it seems that Lake Forest is largely untouched by the turmoil in the world-at-large. Yet, I know that we have the same problems here as any big city in any part of the United States.

You may have read about Mayor Daley's sabotaged speech a little over a year ago at Lake Forest College. He had been invited to speak to government students at the college about the problems of municipal government. Meanwhile, some students also invited comedian Dick Gregory to speak on the same issues. So Daley canceled, and Gregory ending up speaking for about forty minutes on many contemporary issues.

Just to give you an idea of how seriously people are taking race issues here, a local fair housing committee has been formed and is working on integrating Negroes into our North Shore suburbs. The executive director of the fair housing committee was quoted in the paper as saying, "A Negro should be able to go into a realtor's office and be shown the same houses anyone else is. We'll be training escorts to accompany prospective Negroes to real estate offices and homes for sale." Strange, isn't it, to think that this is something that has to be legislated. That we can't figure this out on our own.

I notice that my writing students are tackling these issues more and more in their writing. I encourage them to do so. We need stories to hold up to ourselves as a mirror for the way we live. Yet many people are threatened by words and stories; they don't want to look in the mirror. Perhaps they're afraid of what they might see reflected back.

Yours, C

January 1, 1969

Dear Sam,

Another year gone by. Time speeds up as I get older. James just walked by and asked me if I was writing down my resolutions. And I realized, with a start, that he has absolutely no idea that I write these letters. Do all marriages harbor such secrets? I imagine it would be very disturbing to him to know about these letters, yet I feel entitled to have this part of myself that is separate from my family life. As a matter of fact, it goes beyond entitlement; it is an imperative.

A thought just occurred to me. What if I suddenly died,

and James came upon these unsent letters? Would he open
them and read them, or would he put them in a box,
unopened and mail them to you? What would I do if the
tables were turned? I'd like to think I would send them on,
but I can't be sure what I'd do.

I never really thought of this act of writing to you as having consequences in other people's lives. Of course, their
ultimate and original purpose was to be read by you some
day. But the act of writing them goes beyond that somehow.
I don't know if I can even explain it. It's almost as though I
am no longer writing them for you, but for myself.

When I started writing to you so long ago, forty years ago,
to be exact, my sole purpose was to pour out my heart, and
my love. Then, when we were re-united at some point in our
lives, to let you read the letters. Which, I thought at the
time, would be a matter of a recorded year's worth of yearning and separation.

Yet even after all these years I find myself somehow
unable to sever this connection. Do I really think that some
day you will read these letters, and that they will mean something to you? Or is it enough just to have the connection, as
it exists, in my own mind? My own internal lifeline to something greater than my own life.

Many, many years ago, I did transfer the letters from a
hatbox to a small blue suitcase that locks. I wear the key on
a silver chain around my neck, along with a locket that James
gave me when Jimmy was born. James has never asked me
what the key went to. Although Julie once did when she was
about eleven, and I told her that it was the key to my heart.
Perhaps James thinks it is just a decorative piece of jewelry.
Or perhaps he has never noticed it. There are so many
things we never talk about in our marriage; it is our habit not
to discuss things outside of our daily comings-and-goings.

There is so much about me that James doesn't know, but
that fact no longer seems to hold the importance it once did.

Sometimes I find that whole sentences about my life are formed in my head; that I would like to speak to him about, but that's where they stay — in my head — until I put them down on paper to you. I've always been able to tell you what I can't put into words to James.

I can't say that I haven't tried. In the past I tried to share my interests and dreams with him. But he never seemed to be actively listening. He never offered anything back of his own. It is not his way to talk about inner lives. He is an exterior person who functions in the world of the present. Whereas I live much of my life in my head. I don't blame him for our lack of communication. I'm sure it must not be that easy for him to live with someone who is distracted, overly emotional, and who suddenly has to excuse herself from dinner conversation to write down a line to a poem or a story idea on any available scrap of paper.

Speaking of story ideas, I slowly continue to work on my novel. I haven't told anyone else except Lydia about it, and so far I have only outlined it in one of my notebooks. The seed of it has grown slowly over the past several years, but I wasn't sure what form it would take. I'm still not sure if it will go anywhere. Using the seed metaphor, right now the idea is little more than a tender green stalk. However, the voice of the main character, Claire, steadily lives in me, telling me her life. It is pure imagination fueled by whatever I know of life.

I wonder if it is that way with painters. Do you have an image or a voice that calls to you in dreams to get it down — to get it right? I feel a great responsibility to this voice — to Claire — a responsibility to get it right.

My central idea is to set down the story of an average woman and how she balances her family/exterior life with her creative/interior life. I know it doesn't sound like the stuff of high drama. It doesn't have the sexy cachet that, say, a Philip Roth story would have. Nevertheless I am going to fool with it some more and see what happens. Beginning a novel is like starting out on a journey without an itinerary. You need to be brave and a little foolhardy, but it does leave you open to adventure. If you are like me and find your adventure on the printed page...

I am very proud of a student of mine, Jane Kendall, whom I believe I mentioned before. She wrote a very good short story in my writing class that just won a local fiction contest. It is called *The Nurse's Aide*, and is loosely based on an event that happened in Lake Forest this past year. In her story two young women get the name of an abortionist, a nurse's aide (or so the abortionist is purported to be). They meet at a small motel on the outskirts of town, and go through the abortions. Nearly immediately afterward both young women become ill, and the abortionist's name comes out into the open. It turns out that she is indeed a nurse's aide, in the doctor's office of a prominent physician who is against abortion.

The real events of the story were not exactly as Jane laid them out in her story; but the story she wrote was very true-to-life and very topical. There seems to be a strong trend toward analyzing social trends in fiction. Fiction held up as a mirror to society to view itself from a slight distance. Jane's story doesn't preach one view or the other on abortion; but it makes the reader feel uneasy. It's disturbing in that she challenges both sides of the abortion issue, an issue that seems to be moving to the forefront of the women's movement.

This past Christmas we had Rose and Sarah and their husbands and children all visiting. Everyone is well and happy, and I find being a grandmother to be very satisfying in a way that motherhood never was. In my mind I always fought the confines of motherhood, while at the same time I felt compelled by duty to spend every waking moment with my children. I am not as resistant to being "grandma."

As ever, Catherine

January 1, 1970

Dear Sam,

It seems like the worst kind of necessity that our woman's club has once more been called upon to send holiday gifts to overseas soldiers. Some experiences in life are most pleasurable to repeat, but sending cards and gifts to boys fighting in a war far away is not one of those. Last fall Margaret received a list of twenty names from a friend's son who is serving in an infantry unit in Vietnam. They were names of young men who never receive anything at all from the States. In the same letter he said that they live on C rations, so that boxes of tinned foods and candies are very welcome.

Meanwhile, even as we wrapped gifts for those men on the list, we were reminded of the war in more immediate ways. Students in our local high school and colleges are staging peaceful protests against the war, calling our actions in Vietnam "immoral, illegal and not in the best national interest" (that quote from Professor Jonathan Galloway of Lake Forest College).

All of this was brought home in the worst way when the nephew of one of the ladies in the woman's club came back home last month blinded, from an explosion from a booby trap in South Vietnam.

I don't know if it is my age, or the age we live in, dear Sam, but it seems that there are more issues dividing our country today than at any other time in recent history. I'm excluding the civil war of course, and limiting my discussion to our lifetime.

Besides the war there is the divisive issue of women's rights. There are race riots continuing to plague both our cities and small towns. Even sex itself is an issue. In our own community we have had great controversy over sex education in the schools, and abortion rights. And a new play I saw recently in Chicago, *The Boys in the Band*, even presents homosexuality in a way that will surely make some people upset.

Lydia and I went to a symposium on women's rights this past fall at Barat College here in Lake Forest, along with one of my writing students, Jane Kendall, and some of her friends. They are all well-educated young women in their twenties, some married, some unmarried.

There was a panel of three women representing the women's liberation movement moderating the discussion, along with one male author, the anthropologist Lionel Tiger, who wrote *Men in Groups*, a recent best seller.

The evidence presented by Mr. Tiger's studies pointed to women's inferior position in many cultures, where they have traditionally held the subordinate role in society. Men, of course being the dominant force in politics, business, war, and religion.

Dr. Mary Ellman, a literary critic and author on the panel replied that, "In the past, marriage for a woman meant a succession of hazardous pregnancies and the risk of death in childbirth. We most certainly owe Jane Austen's novels to her life-long virginity. And we don't know how many Jane Austens died before they wrote a word."

That comment really hit me hard. I thought back on my own life, and the lives of most women I know, and tried to analyze why we made the choices we made, mainly to put husbands and family first, and our own ambitions and needs on the back burner.

One young mother stood up and told a story of her six-year-old daughter who had recently told her that when she grew up she was going to be a nurse. The mother replied that perhaps she might want to be a doctor instead. To which her little girl replied, "I can't be a doctor. I'm a girl."

I'm not sure what to think. I don't look at men as the

enemy, but I do see the point that women are living in a male dominated culture and some things need to change.

Change. That word seems to be the by-word of this new decade we are entering. So many things we have lived with as a nation and as individuals are being called into question. And not just in the privacy of our homes or even our communities, but on the streets, loudly and vehemently, and often violently.

I'm trying to put some of these feelings into my writing, especially in the book I'm working on. I know I have always had feminist tendencies, but mostly I've kept those thoughts to myself, or written them here. Perhaps I can give those feelings a voice in my work.

If *your* feelings are given a voice in your work, then surely you have an inner life full of passion and beauty, as evidenced by the photo spread your work received in *Arizona Highways*. They did a stunning job of reproducing your paintings; your images jump off the page and into the heart. I'm proud to know you.

Sometimes I feel very eccentric for having harbored this secret passion in my heart of hearts all these years, yet I have lived a full and wonderful life. In my book, Claire loses her fiancé in World War I, yet goes on to marry and have a family. She never forgets the great love of her life for a single day, yet she is able to go forward in her life and find happiness. I believe that the knowledge of the possibility of great love sustains us all.

As ever, Catherine

P. S. I haven't written about the Inn for a long while. It continues to be the hub of our little town, especially for special occasions such as the following:

... ...

Enjoy the dignified atmosphere of the Forest Inn for your next group activity. We have delightful facilities available to handle from 20 to 150 people. We feature fine American cuisine with a European touch.

* *Book Reviews*
* *Bridge Parties*
* *Prom Dinners*
* *Business Clubs*
* *Service Clubs*
* *Wedding Receptions*
* *Teas*

... ...

A Home-like Christmas Dinner at the Forest Inn
* *Chef's Suggestion* *

*

Cream of Fresh Mushroom Soup
*

Molded Fruit Christmas Salad
*

Special Christmas Turkey with Celery Dressing, Giblet Gravy, Cranberry Sauce
*

Green Peas & Snowflake Potatoes
*

Pumpkin Pie with Whipped Cream
*

Coffee or tea

*

$4.75

January 1, 1971

Dear Sam,

As I sit down to record the previous year, I hardly know where to begin. It's always an interesting exercise to sum up a year of one's life in a few short paragraphs. I find even as I get older (my sixtieth birthday was this past September), my interest in politics remains strong. In fact, instead of retreating into my own world as many women my age seem to do, I become more interested in the world around me with the passing of each year.

I have never felt my age more keenly though as I did this past March when Lydia and I crammed into the Highland Park High School auditorium with about 1,600 other people (1,200 more sat in the gymnasium listening on a speaker) to hear Chicago Seven defendant Rennie Davis. He talked about the older generation (that's you and me, dear) as one that finds military solutions to social problems, and said that the 70's are going to be a trial of the younger generation. I'd like to see what happens when his generation of political leaders is faced with some of the same issues as Vietnam—will they fare any better? Are "military solutions" a generational reaction to a crisis, or does it go much deeper than that to a cultural and gender level?

Davis's speech was sponsored by the North Shore Women for Peace, and the president of the group said that an anonymous phone caller had awakened her at 4:30 that morning threatening to burn down her house if Davis's speech was allowed to go on.

It was frightening, yet strangely exciting to hear Davis. His speech was liberally sprinkled with obscenities, yet he said that the real obscenity is our government's policy in Vietnam. I remember he said this, "The young people of this country are determined to take this country back from the Nixons, Agnews, Hayakawas, Daleys, and Reagans by any means necessary."

Two weeks later I went to see the Reverend Jesse Jackson speaking here at Barat College. There were about five hundred of us there, a pretty good crowd for a chilly, dismal evening. He's heading up an organization called Operation Breadbasket, and his talk was sponsored by the Panel of American Women with the cooperation of clergy and churches in Lake Forest and Lake Bluff. I wrote down some of his speech in a journal, because I knew Sarah would want to know everything he said. Most important, I think, was his statement, "America's white man lives in a superior illusion which has forced the black man into an inferior delusion. We have to make a stand for that which is right, even though it's painful, before it's too late."

It seems that everyone in America feels disenfranchised.

Thank God I have Lydia, and sometimes my former writing student Jane to go with to all these events. James would no more go to a talk by Jesse Jackson than he would make snow angels in the front yard.

Which brings me to the next political event, which we attended in April. Lydia, Jane, and I paid twenty-five dollars a plate to attend a dinner in Highland Park as a fundraiser for Adlai E. Stevenson III, for U. S. senator, and James J. Cone, for U. S. representative. I must confess to you, though, that perhaps our main interest wasn't in meeting the political candidates. The featured speaker was actor Warren Beatty. Mr. Beatty was a personal friend of Cone's — they had gone to Northwestern together.

He looked different in person than he did in *Bonnie and Clyde*, although we had to keep reminding ourselves that we weren't there for that... He had a beard and mustache and long, sort of shaggy hair and black frame glasses. Very charming and handsome, nonetheless.

I repeated something Mr. Beatty said later to James, who didn't seem to grasp the connection, or why I was telling him, "I don't think it's possible to be uninvolved with politics," said Mr. Beatty. "If you're uninvolved there, you're uninvolved, period." Beatty didn't pass himself off as any kind of political genius; he merely recognized the attention his being there would attract, and took advantage of it for his candidate.

Are you ready for more politics? As a result of her prize-winning short story with the abortion theme, Jane was asked to join a panel of North Shore women to speak on the topic "Abortion: Freedom to Choose." As part of her research for serving on the panel, she found out that it is estimated that at least fifty thousand illegal abortions are performed annually in Illinois. Many of the young women who have these illegal abortions die or become very ill from improper medical care. As one of the women on the panel remarked, "The female uterus is the only part of the human body that is legislated." Another woman stated her position, "I am not for abortions, but I am against more unwanted children."

I view my role in all of this as being that of an interested and informed citizen. I have daughters and grandchildren; and I don't want to become a doddering old biddy who has no clue what is going on in the world. I may not march in the streets, but I can listen to those who do, and be open to new ideas.

You would think that, living in a small town in the Midwest, much of the world would pass us by, leaving us untouched. But I have never found that to be the case. We felt what happened at Kent State as keenly as though it had happened at our own Lake Forest College. I'm still in shock and despair that this happened in our great nation. My father would have been proud of the students at Lake Forest College who staged a strike to protest the war and the death of the Kent State students.

This past year has been marked by two images in my mind: silent vigils with candles illuminating young, fearful faces; and marchers with mouths open wide, screaming their pain to the world.

I will now write of something besides the political upheavals that are affecting us all. In February I got to sit in on an interview at the Forest Inn with poet William Snodgrass. I acted as a hostess, eavesdropping shamelessly until Mr. Snodgrass politely asked me to sit down and join him and his interviewer. He was the poet-in-residence last year at Lake Forest College, and he gave several lectures that were open to the public.

I thought of you during his lecture "Poems About Paintings," in which he discussed his poem about Van Gogh's *Starry Night* and four other poems he has written about paintings. It got me to thinking that that would be a good exercise for me — to write a poem about one of your paintings, perhaps the one I keep above my desk.

He also spoke of his Pulitzer Prize-winning book of poems, *Heart's Needle,* and of other poets he has known and studied. He said something interesting about Robert Frost that I have never heard before. He said, "The ladies club members think he is a grand old patriarch — pastoral and gentle. Actually, when you get beneath the surface of his work you find a terrifying man. I couldn't live with his empty cold view of the world for a minute. T. S. Eliot is cuddly compared to Robert Frost."

I must write next year of other things. I do continue to work on my novel, although I alternate between hating it, and thinking it might be mediocre at best. I put it away for long stretches of time, hoping it will leave me alone. I work on other things, as my growing stacks of notebooks will attest to, but Claire refuses to leave me alone. I hear her voice in my dreams, and she is my mother, my mother's lost mother, Lydia, Sarah, Rose, Julie, and myself.

The world is so sad and angry; will it always be so from this time forward?

Yours, C

January 1, 1972

Dear Sam,

You may call me *Ms.* Caldwell... Will this someday be known as the year women raised their collective voices? And not in unity, either. There are so many facets to the whole concept of women's liberation; it is impossible to pigeonhole the movement itself as representing one thing, or one idea.

Some see the movement as centered on abortion rights, and indeed in my community the attempt to legalize abortion in the Illinois legislature has been the topic of much heated controversy.

Others see the movement only as financially motivated — equal pay for equal work and that sort of thing. Others want simply to raise awareness of women, so women don't see being a housewife as the only option in their life. Still others see men as oppressors, granted their status by history, and unwilling to change the status quo.

I had a wonderful opportunity to hear Gloria Steinem speak in Highland Park last February. I couldn't help wonder whether her gorgeous, feminine appearance works against her feminism. Which is silly, because why should she look like a frump just to prove she is a feminist spokesperson?

I took lots of notes, and here are some of the highlights quoted from her, from my notebook:

... *"All through school, we were taught only white, male history."*

... *"Women are often maintained as ornaments or children and sometimes as servants. A man will often marry a woman he wouldn't think of as bright enough to hire."*

... *"A woman is considered as good at detail work, as long as it's poorly paid factory work; but when it comes to brain surgery, she's not so good anymore."*

... *"We must stop saying 'be a doctor' to one child, and 'marry a doctor' to another child."*

... *"In the long-run, women's liberation will be men's liberation too."*

... *"Only one bra has been burned during the movement, and that was during the 1968 Miss America National Meat Market Contest."*

In my own world, James is remodeling the Inn, and basically living there full time.

I am spending much of my time writing, and still teaching writing classes at Gorton.

My book is at a dead end, but I keep working.

I think of you often, and wonder if you ever think of me.

Yours, Ms. C

P. S. A poem, now that I am old, about an even older woman I overheard talking to her daughter.

The Weight of Things

"I don't want to be a burden,"
Says the old woman with hair
The color of milk.
Her larynx bobs like a baby bird's
Drawing nourishment from the air
To float tremulous voice
That once sang soprano in the choir.

I know her—
The one thing that tells you
Who she was
Are her eyes, clear blue
As the mountain lake she swam across as a girl.
And it's someone else's hands that are trembling.

When I consider burdens, it's not this
A burden would be empty hands
With no sweater to button straight.
Or not hearing that still-sweet warble
Crooning to the birds at the feeder
When she thinks no one is listening.

January 1, 1973

Dearest, dearest Sam,

How difficult it is to write to you instead of being there in person sharing your life at this very difficult time. Mandy's death from the long-term effects of her polio wasn't a complete shock, but even when we have some foreshadowing of death, it is not any easier to bear. She was a strong, loving woman, and I'm happy you had her in your life as wife and mother, if not as your heart's heart.

Perhaps I should have left right after the funeral, rather than extending my stay. After all, the excuse of wanting to visit Sarah, Charlie, Julie, and Drake was just that, an excuse. I had my own selfish reasons, I'll admit. I was experiencing my own sort of breakdown, a crisis of confidence and faith in my own life that I should not have burdened you with at that particular time, when you were so vulnerable. Neither one of us was in a normal state of mind, although those two weeks sustain me now as I write to you.

How strange it felt to sit with you alone in the ranch house after all the time that has passed since we were young and so passionately in love. Amanda gone, our children all grown, your parents and mine gone as well. I felt like we were two survivors from a shipwreck, clinging to each other to keep from drowning.

Those first days and nights after the funeral passed in a blur with family and friends coming and going. Then suddenly, everyone had gone home, and it was just you and I sitting with our feet up in front of a blazing fire. It felt completely natural, yet every minute that ticked by seemed precious and rare, because I knew it couldn't stay that way.

Life is so strange. I would have thought that by the time I was this age, my emotions and feelings would be settled and controlled, and that I would be content to sit on a rocking chair and crochet afghans for my grandchildren. *Au contraire.*

Instead, when I found myself alone with you, all the years between us didn't seem to matter. What mattered was the moment.

How easy it was to slip back into the habit of loving you. You know that, my dearest Sam. And to find out that you had never stopped loving me all those years... What a wondrous revelation. Even as I sit here now surrounded by the howling winds of a prairie winter, I can close my eyes and breathe in your scent, along with the smell of horses and leather and sage and pine.

I think we both knew, even as we began, that it would have to end. As much as I pride myself on being attuned to the freedoms offered by feminism, I have been too strongly molded by my own times. I simply don't have the strength and selfishness it would take to divorce James. He has been a good husband, and it would destroy him and my family if we were to divorce now. I can't, in good moral conscience do that to him.

I have lived in Lake Forest my whole life, and as much as Sedona is a place I visit often in my dreams, I can't imagine leaving my home and my history behind. I may be an adventuress on the page, but I guess when it comes to real life, I am not so brave. You said that I could keep my home here and we could return as often as I liked to visit, but I fear that wouldn't be the same. I feel like I'm part of a story, that story being my own unfolding history here in Lake Forest. And I want to stay and see how the story turns out.

I know that I am free now to write you as I please, so these secret missives no longer hold the importance they once did. And I know through our correspondence over this past year that we will always have the most remarkable bond a man and woman can have together. I love you deeply, my dearest Sam, but my love goes beyond the need to be next to you, in your physical presence. It is a spiritual love, a kinship of soul that will sustain me. I only hope that you can find the same sustenance.

Our situation brings to mind a talk I went to last year before I came out to Mandy's funeral. I'm sure you've heard of the diaries published by Anais Nin, who at sixty-eight is actually older than I am. I came away from her lecture thinking about how independent she has been in her life; how she never cared about what others thought. She was muse and lover and teacher and nurturer, always on her own terms. She said that women have traditionally been restricted to a small world, but because of this developed a special intuition for human relationships. Then she remarked that now was the time for women to move out of this small world, and into the larger one. "It is time for women to reveal themselves," she said.

I realized that by writing — these letters, my notebooks, my poems, my stories — I am revealing myself in the only way I know how. I am no Anais Nin or Gloria Steinem; out in the world, shaping life as one would an unformed lump of clay. Rather it is through my written record that I live a life outside of my own. I'm not one to shout from the rooftops or hop on a train to Sedona and take up a new life. I take what is in my heart and put it on paper. I release it, and offer it to whoever will take it.

Your heart's heart, C

February 14, 1973

Old Man...

...When you come up behind me that way
While I'm slicing apples for pie
At the kitchen counter
And you nuzzle my neck with your beard
And I feel your breath hot on my shoulder.

The years slip off us like our clothes
Which are somehow on the counter
Folded neatly; I do remember hearing
The clink of your belt buckle.

The rest of it is like it always is;
Quivering disbelief that it is so
The astounding luck of it, the fate
That we willed to happen through desire.

That desire is forever an ocean
That marks its tides in my soul
And you are the moon I hold
In my orbit, hanging full over me.

My love, I grasp your gray head to me
Our faces inches apart, eyes lost in eyes
I smell the salts of that ocean
And cinnamon for the pie that waits patiently for us.

June 14, 1973

Dear Sam,

I'm not sure why you have sent back my letters from the last several months unopened. Sarah reports that everyone is worried about you; that you have moved out of the main house and down to the cabin by the creek, and that you are spending all your time painting.

I know all too well that desire to create which arises out of other needs, but I worry that you are having some sort of breakdown. My instinct tells me you are not a man to live on his own, and that you must be lonely beyond imagining with your children grown, Mandy gone, and then losing what hopes you harbored all these years that we might somehow find a way to be together.

Your last letter caused me such pain. I know you can't understand why I don't leave James. I don't know how I can explain it any better than to tell you that it goes against every-thing I have lived my life as. It is who I am. I don't try to justify myself, I don't say it is any less painful for me, and I can't offer a logical explanation.

I'm not brave and fearless. I can't leave James. The habit and commitment of marriage is a harder chain to break than I ever considered. To turn my back on all those years is to admit failure, and to say that my life has been a sham. What could I tell James? That I never loved him as a wife should love her husband? That there is so much more of me he doesn't know? I don't regret what you and I shared when I was at the ranch after Mandy's funeral. And I sincerely don't think I made any promises to you at that time. We both knew what we were doing, which doesn't make this situ-ation any easier, I know.

My writing has always made up for that part of me that

James never reached. I always had that outlet and still do.

I suspect and hope you are doing the same with your painting right now—using it to fill those spaces that no one else can reach.

Worryingly, C

January 1, 1975

Dearest Sam,

I am pacing the floor of my small study here, once Sarah's room, debating whether or not to send you this entire bundle of letters from these past decades. Since you won't answer my real, sent letters, perhaps these would serve as a sort of explanation for my actions. Dear, dear Sam... it breaks my heart that you are so alone. True, you do have the ranch, and there are people there who care for you greatly. But at this time of your life, with Mandy gone and your children grown, I am certain the loneliness must be crushing. I know, because I have lived with that loneliness inside of me most of my life. I have never felt my interior life matched my exterior life. For some people that would be debilitating. I learned to accept it a long time ago, and I let that interior life come out through my imagination in my writing. It sounds like you are trying to do that with your painting right now. I hope you find some measure of peace.

Lovingly, Catherine

P. S. The darkness of grief and loneliness affects everyone so differently. I'm thinking of the poet Anne Sexton, whose work and life I have followed with interest for years now. How sad that she had to take her own life the way she did.

January 1, 1976

Dear Sam,

Somehow I resisted the urge last year to send you these letters. I'm not sure why. I guess I thought they might be too much for you to handle in your emotional state.

And now that you have remarried this past July, I will keep them locked here, in this small suitcase. I sincerely hope you will find peace and happiness with Grace, Amanda's sister. I remember when Grace's husband died about ten years ago. If I recall correctly he was the one who was kicked in the head by a wild horse. And it is certainly natural for two people who are lonely to be drawn to one another for comfort and company.

Is there a warped irony that so shortly after your marriage, James became ill and died so quickly? It is hard to imagine people can still die of something as simple as pneumonia in this day of advanced medical care. And even though he was seventy years old, now that I am nearly that same age, seventy no longer seems old.

I have decided to sell the Inn. It was James' life, not mine, and I don't have the drive to oversee it and keep it in the family. I met with Sarah and Rose after the funeral and they were in agreement with me; neither of them had an interest in running it or keeping it in our family. It feels like the end of an era. I am fairly certain the new owners, a consortium of business people from Chicago, will preserve the heritage and structural integrity that makes the Inn such an integral part of our community.

So, my dear Sam... Now I am free to do with my life as I wish, and you are embarking on your own new life. Sarah writes that she and Charlie will be overseeing the ranch while you and Grace travel for the next year.

Perhaps travel would be a good antidote for the heaviness in my own heart right now. Yes, I believe I will at least travel to California to see Bridget. California in January is certainly much more pleasant than this frigid gray place. I can take Lydia with me, and we'll both warm ourselves, and see flowers blooming, and by the time I return to Illinois, the sky will be blue again, and I will be able to sit in James' garden.

Yours, Catherine

P. S. Thank you again for yours and Grace's condolences. And I truly am glad, Sam, that you found your way out of a very dark place; the same place I am trying not to slide into myself.

January 1, 1979

Dear Sam,

I think it has been one or two years since I last wrote you one of these private missives. If you and Grace have been receiving my postcards, you know that I have been spending my winters in southern California these past years.

The year after James died and you remarried I drifted aimlessly from day to day. I was never a person to give in to feeling sorry for myself, and unlike many creative types, I've never experienced debilitating mood swings. The worst time I ever had in my life was after Jimmy died, but I learned to live with that loss much as one would learn to live with a missing limb. Not a day goes by that I don't think of him, but I have had to accept that terrible loss and go on with life.

I guess I have always been a person who, when presented with problems in life has turned them into challenges instead. Problems always seem a bit like a puzzle to me; they are something to be solved, and I work them over in my brain until I can reach some sort of satisfaction.

But when I last wrote to you, I started to sink down to that place where I had been when Jimmy died, when everything seemed false and pointless. I lost my connection with anything meaningful in my life. I couldn't even read or write. I couldn't sit still, nor could I focus on anything. All I seemed to do was wander my house, going from room to room with a cup of tea.

I was miserably tiresome company, I'm afraid.

Then one day Lydia fell on a patch of ice when going out to get the mail, and she broke her collarbone. As she needed to remain immobile as much as possible, and was in pain, I suggested she move in with me temporarily, into the spare bedroom. And there she has been ever since.

And the most marvelous thing came out of her fall (that does sound terrible, I know, that her fall turned out to be a good thing). On her doctor's suggestion, we went to southern California, so that she could heal in a milder climate, and while we were there Lydia bought a small beach bungalow in Laguna Beach. She sold her home here in Lake Forest, and for the past three years we have spent our winters in Laguna. Actually she goes there in November and stays until May. I have been going from January until March, allowing each of us some private time. Even the best of "roomies" can use some space apart.

Laguna Beach has been a revelation. A person could not go there in winter and be depressed. The quality of light, the vivid abundance of flowers, the brilliant sky, the sunsets, the eucalyptus trees, and even the quirky people make it all a complete change of pace. Lydia spends much of her time studying the California Impressionists who painted there around the turn of the century and during the early 20's and 30's. And I find myself fascinated by them also.

So here we are, two doddering old ladies, trotting down to

the beach every day, Lydia with her sketchbooks and sometimes her paints and easel, and myself with notebooks, pens,
and books.

I'm quite enjoying this phase of my life. For the first
time I have no one to take care of but myself. It took me a
couple of years to admit that, and it is just now feeling
"right." Most women fall so naturally into the role of care-
taker, that the role becomes our identity. Lydia, never having
married, never had to make that adjustment. Except for the
short time she had to care for her mother, she has always
pleased only herself. How rare it is to do the same.

In fact as soon as I finish this letter, I will begin to close
up my house here. I leave for Laguna in two days. It has
been very hectic the past two weeks. Sarah and Rose visited
here with their families over the holidays—it was the first
time we have all been together in the last few years. Julie,
who is now twenty-five and engaged to a young man from
Colorado, was there, and so were Rose's two sons.

I miss Lake Forest when I am gone, but find that the winters here are just too severe, and that when you are my age
the less one has to deal with howling winds, ice, and snow
drifts, the better. During the summers I still go for long
walks on the Shaw prairie, and love sitting by the lake in the
sun. I no longer feel the intense pain I used to knowing that
the lake is where Jimmy died. The lake seems like a thing
unto itself, an immovable force of nature. Our own lives are
so inconsequential and transient when compared to things
like lakes and canyons and stars and prairies.

I have recently begun taking notes again for the novel I
was working on before James died. It has a name now. It is
called *The Lake Poet*, and I am working steadily on it. I have
no idea what I will do with it, or if it is publishable, but
something compels me to write it. Oddly, it sometimes feels
like it is the main reason I was put on this earth.

I get such inspiration from meeting with and listening to

talks by other women writers, and even in my darkest days after James died, I would leave the house for that one thing. The ones I recall best from the past several years are Margaret Atwood, a Canadian poet and novelist who was the poet-in-residence at Lake Forest College a year or two back; and also Judith Guest, the author of *Ordinary People*. She was in town recently reading and signing her book at the Lake Forest library. The town is abuzz over her announcement that Robert Redford has bought the film rights to her book and that he might film it here. He was actually in Lake Forest briefly a little while back, and you would have thought President Carter was here, with all the excitement! Robert Altman's film *A Wedding* just finished filming at the Armour estate, and Kirk Douglas was here for a day filming a scene for a movie at our beach. I have seen more movie stars right here in Market Square than I ever saw in southern California!

I hope you and yours are all well. Sarah keeps me filled in. It sounds like you are traveling and working as well. I'm anxious to see your latest paintings. I must call the gallery in Sedona and ask them to send me some photographs.

Your fellow footloose wanderer, C

January 1, 1980

Dearest Sam,

Strange to be writing this from sunny Laguna Beach. And also amazing to find a new decade suddenly before us. I just realized that it is entirely possible that we might be alive to see the millennium. I only hope my mental capacities are such that I'll know what is happening then. Sometimes I wonder what this last part of my life has in store for me. When I'm around my grandchildren it seems impossible that

I was ever that young, or that my own children were that young. The decisions young people are faced with are so very different from the ones of my generation. There were so few opportunities for women in 1929, for example, as compared to today. Or perhaps the opportunities were there — I just wasn't aware of them, or lacked the ambition or courage to look further than my backyard fence.

Sarah wrote to me that you and Grace were barely back from your trip to Europe before you left on a tour of Asia. I must say, I envy your ability to take off and travel. I had always thought I would do so at this age, but right now I am very content to go between Laguna Beach and Lake Forest. I am reading and re-reading as many of the great women writers as I can. I feel this need to immerse myself in great literature by women in order to find my own true voice. For the past several years I have been studying Virginia Woolf, May Sarton, Katherine Ann Porter, Jane Austen, and Emily Dickinson, to name a few. I have written of this before, but I still find it to be very revealing that none of these particular women writers had traditional families — husband, children, in-laws, etc. It makes me even more determined to give a voice to Claire, the woman in my novel-in-progress, *The Lake Poet*. Surely women with families and ordinary lives have stories too.

I continue also with my poetry. Since poetry is woven into Claire's story in *The Lake Poet*, I feel constantly challenged to improve my own work in this area. Some of my most important inspiration still comes from attending poetry readings, and when I'm in Lake Forest, Lydia and I try to go to everything we can. I particularly enjoyed Galway Kinnell when he was at the college a year or so ago, and then, just recently Denise Levertov, who was poet-in-residence in November at Lake Forest College.

The most exciting news, though, is that Robert Redford and his film crew were in Lake Forest this past fall filming

Judith Guest's bestseller *Ordinary People*. Normally sane
people were in a frenzy trying to "run into" him in town, and
also the stars Mary Tyler Moore and Donald Sutherland.
When the movie comes out, you must look closely at the part
where a crowd is coming out of a movie theater. Lydia and I
were selected as extras for this one scene; they used many
Lake Foresters in the movie. It was very exciting at first, but
you wouldn't believe how long we had to wait around just to
walk out the "theater" door (it was really our town recreation
center). "What you do as an extra is wait," Mr. Redford had
warned us, before the scene was shot. But none of us really
cared. I never thought I would be one to be star struck, but
Lydia and I agreed that there is something about Bob (as we
have taken to calling him) that makes a person dizzy in his
presence. Men are not immune to this either, it would seem.
They were jockeying to be around him just as much as the
women. He is very handsome, but shorter than I thought he
would be. I think his movie will be very good.

As I've mentioned through the years, our little corner of
the prairie has always been a cultural hub for literary and
artistic events. I'm not sure what it is that attracts some of
the best creative minds, because, really Lake Forest is just
small town America. I have a feeling that this heritage will
continue even more strongly because now our town can boast
a real retreat for writers and artists.

I believe I told you many years ago about Ragdale, the
home of the Howard Van Doren Shaw family. The home sits
on one of the last undeveloped prairies in this part of Illinois,
and is a rambling, cozy place in the Arts and Crafts style that
you would fall in love with if you saw it. The remaining Shaw
family members have decided to set Ragdale up as a resi-
dence for artists and writers, and already there are people
working there and holding classes in poetry and fiction writing. Quite marvelous, when you think about it...

I am not as active in the Woman's Club as I once was, but

every now and then I do get involved in some project with that group of dear friends. I was thinking though, that throughout the years so many of our efforts have dealt with the side effects of war. Even today. I'm thinking of a recent event our club held in North Chicago. We held a picnic for veterans there; so sad to see so many forgotten men. Men to whom the most important event of their lives was one war or another. War uses people up and tosses them aside, broken and forgotten.

I don't know why, but sometimes still I spy a young man in a crowd, or an anonymous passerby, and if he has a certain way of carrying himself, or a lopsided smile, I think of Jimmy with a clarity that leaves me dizzy. I miss him every day of my life. And you, as well, my dearest.

Yours, Catherine

January 1, 1981

Dear Sam,

Lydia just asked me what I was writing, and I told her I was writing you a letter; that I write you a letter every year at this time. I didn't mention to her, though, that I never mail these letters. Some things remain private even among the closest of friends. Lately, though, I have been thinking of what, indeed, I will do with these letters. I would like you to have them, and I completely trust that you would accept them in the spirit they were written in. However, I feel as though it would be inappropriate for Grace to read them, and I wouldn't want to put you in the position of having to hide anything from her. So, here is my plan. I have decided that I will give these to you at the millennium—in the year 2000, no matter what our situations. By then we will all be too old to get upset with anyone over past or imagined hurts. We can just accept what was and be glad we shared what we had in our hearts all these years.

And if one of us dies before then (yes, I realize that is the more likely scenario), then I will leave a provision in my will for my granddaughter Julie to take possession of these letters and do what she thinks is best with them. I have also been trying to decide what to do with all of my notebooks and papers and poems and stories, and my novel-in-progress *The Lake Poet*. Elizabeth Harding, the woman who published my chapbook of poems, assures me that Midwest Press will publish it. Although I fear that an old-fashioned, poetic novel about unrequited love, with no sex or violence in it will have a very limited audience in today's literary marketplace.

I write this sitting in my little room in Laguna Beach, where the sound of the ocean and the warmth of the sun soothe and nourish me. I have grown to love this winter refuge, although I hear in the summer it is dreadfully overrun with tourists. I wish I could have seen it as the early California Impressionist painters did — Lydia and I study their work and see in their paintings a world no longer in existence. Perhaps that is one reason art is so valuable. It is a real record or impression of images that may never be seen again in that exact way, only imagined through the artist's eyes.

In May, Lydia and Jane and I and several of Jane's friends marched with the North Suburban NOW committee in downtown Chicago. It is simply unbelievable to me that my own state of Illinois, which is so progressive in other areas, is so backward that the state legislature has not passed the Equal Rights Amendment. I am working on a poem about the march, because the image of women, all wearing white, marching for their beliefs, stays in my mind. It brings to my mind a twin image of the women suffragettes marching for the vote in their white linen dresses so many years ago.

Our days here in Laguna are simple, yet peaceful and fulfilling. The climate here is marvelous, and the quality of
light is the best in the United States for painting, according
to Lydia. Not that anyone will ever know that but me — Lydia
continues to paint and then promptly ships everything home,
and stores the paintings in our attic. I have long ago given
up persuading her to have a show, or enter an art fair, or
even farm some of them out to a local gallery. Her talent is
very authentic, but she thinks her work is amateurish, compared to the great California Impressionists like Guy Rose or
William Wendt.

I compare Lydia to Emily Dickinson, in that apparently
her work will be loved only after she is gone. Although dear
Emily tried to send her work out into the marketplace, whereas Lydia does not. We saw the play *The Belle of Amherst* a
couple of years ago, and I think Lydia recognized in Emily
Dickinson a kindred spirit. I tell Lydia that if she dies before
I do, I'm going to lug all of her paintings out of the attic, put
them on easels on the front lawn of our Lake Forest home,
and invite every gallery owner in Chicago and Laguna Beach
to come see them. I think she would be pleased at such a
thing. It infuriates me, though, that she won't show her work
now. We argue about it vehemently every now and then, but
I have just about given up on ever changing her mind. She
points out that I have not sent much of my work out into the
marketplace either, which I'm afraid is true. All these years
of writing; stacks of notebooks filled with poems and bits of
stories and images, and the only tangible thing I have to
show for it is my small chapbook of poems and one as yet
unpublished novel.

If Elizabeth does take my novel, I know in my heart that
it is the last solid work I will do. I've decided that is perfectly
fine, though. If a person produces one really meaningful
work in his or her life, isn't that enough? In my writing classes, students were always very concerned with producing a

large volume of work. And I'm not denying the appeal of that.

But my reply to them has always been to try to write the one best poem that is in them, or the one best short story. Write all the other ones, too, sure, you have to write and write, and work all the time. But if the one thing you write happens to be: *I think that I shall never see/A poem lovely as a tree*, or *Gone With the Wind* or *The Lottery* or *Stopping by Woods on a Snowy Evening* or *To Kill a Mockingbird*, why, then you have created something of lasting beauty. What more would one want from life?

Obviously, not everyone is cut out to be a writer or artist (thank God), but I believe that each person can cultivate some gift that they are born with, some passion that is unique to them. For some it may be raising a family, others are brilliant at nursing or teaching. The trick is to find the one thing you love doing, pursue it with single-minded passion, and become the best you can at it. I think that is where you can find true happiness and pride and contentment. Perhaps this is where a lot of marriages go wrong. We expect another person to be the thing in life that fulfills us. We put all our expectations on them. If I didn't have *my* grand passion, my writing, to save me I would never have survived my marriage. Words are where I went to fill my soul. Was that right to do? I don't know, even now. Perhaps it was unfair to James that I never loved him as much as he loved me. It seemed to be enough for him, though. I think he respected and admired me and loved me in his quiet way, and understood to a certain extent that we were very different.

I don't know why I am thinking of all these things now. I guess they don't matter much. James is gone, and I have lived most of my life. Oddly, though, it is these moments, when looking out at the infinite blue ocean and sky, that I can so readily travel back in time, and the images are as clear as if they happened yesterday.

You and I may not have had our lives together, as we once planned, but you were with me every day. I loved you with a great love and it vividly colored everything else I did for the rest of my life.

Yours, as ever, Catherine

March 15, 1981

Dear Sam,

You have no idea what it means to me that you sent me a painting to use for the cover of my book *The Lake Poet*. I was surprised and moved beyond words (and for me that is saying something—I always have words!) Luckily I am at a small press, and such creative decisions can be made as we wish. I know at the large publishing houses, a staff artist is assigned to do the cover art, and the writer rarely has any input into how a book will actually be represented artistically.

If you read this someday, you will already have received my heartfelt thanks in a letter I just wrote to you and Grace. But I feel I must record here for you as well, how much this means to me.

Most sincerely, Catherine

January 1, 1982

Dear Sam,

My novel was published this past fall by Midwest Press, and surprisingly it has had some measure of success. I have decided to stay here in Lake Forest this winter, as there have been some promotional events at local bookstores. Julie brought her two little ones out during the holidays, and has decided to stay an extra couple of weeks because her husband is traveling in Europe on business for the month. I am very glad for her company, and that of my two great grandsons.

Midwest Press printed 1,000 copies of *The Lake Poet*, which seems like a lot for a small book. But when you compare it to the huge numbers printed for today's bestsellers, it seems miniscule. Elizabeth sees a trend toward certain "mass market" authors commanding the lion's share of the bestseller list, and even sees a trend toward those authors becoming celebrities like movie stars.

As for my own work, I'm just thrilled I have something tangible to show for all my mental musings and midnight jottings. I'm glad not to be a celebrity author; I had an attack of extreme nerves when I had to do a reading and signing at Lake Forest Book Store, right here in town! It is one of those tiny bookstores, with books crammed into every possible nook and cranny, and barely enough room for my table and chair. There was actually a line out the door at one point, which in reality isn't saying much as only about twenty people can fit in the bookstore at one time. People in Lake Forest have been very supportive of my work, and also curious, knowing that my book was set here. I feel confident that I represented the town well, and happy that I gave voice to my "ordinary" protagonist Claire.

Amazingly, publication of my novel has spurred interest in the chapbook of poems that Midwest Press published some years ago, and they have printed 500 more of those. As I sit behind the tables set up for me at various local bookstores, I feel no different than a peddler selling her wares. I'm just a peddler of words.

Lydia has been in Laguna for the past two months, but will travel to Washington, D. C. for Reagan's inauguration. She still has many journalism cronies there who will do anything for her, including making sure she gets invitations to the gala events that week.

More and more, it seems, politicians and celebrities seem to be overlapping each other's spheres of influence (an actor for President!) I thought of this when I went in October to a benefit for the passage of the ERA at a home here in Lake Forest. Marlo Thomas and Phil Donahue were the celebrity guests, obviously to attract attention and money. More than two hundred of us each paid twenty-five dollars to attend. I guess there is nothing inherently wrong with the concept, but it does make you wonder if people aren't too focused on celebrity for its own sake, rather than the issues.

I was a guest lecturer at a poetry workshop at Ragdale this past fall. I don't know if I will ever get comfortable being seen as an "expert" in the field of writing. When I'm speaking I get the feeling that someone in one of my classes will see through me, and say I don't know any more about writing than anyone else. I don't have my Ph. D., and I've never been part of the academic community. Much of my work has been done in privacy to please and challenge myself.

There is a line a writer crosses at some time in his or her life, and the words you so carefully set down need to be released into the world. It feels egotistical to a certain extent, presuming that anyone else would be interested in what you have to say. You have to either have or develop the necessary drive and ambition to get your work published. The writing part has always come much more easily to me — believing that what I had to say was valid and interesting to others has been the difficult part. I think it is like that more for women writers than for men. Men have always assumed their place in the world; women have had to push themselves out into it. Many can't do so, and I wonder how many wonderful works are hidden in drawers and attics, and even in thoughts that don't make it as far as paper.

I'd forgotten how bitter cold the winters are here, and I

miss Laguna. This will probably be my last winter here, but nothing can keep me away from my beloved Lake Forest during spring, summer, and fall. As beautiful as the Pacific is, I have never found anything as mysterious and wondrous as a full summer moon hanging over Lake Michigan, fireflies flickering their magic lights, and cicadas singing their shrill summer song.

I am lonely today, and even though Julie, Bobby, and Jimmy are here I feel like I'm drifting aimlessly around the house. I miss you and am filled with longing for you. Isn't it silly that at my age I could feel that way? I look in the mirror and see an old woman, but in my heart I feel the same feelings I had as a young woman.

Lately I wake up so early, and as it really is too cold to get up and do anything outdoors, I lie in bed and think back on different times in my life. My times with the children when they were young, and my time with you, my dear Sam, were the happiest times of my life. I always felt so natural and complete with you, and we were able to talk to one another in the most intimate way. I try very hard not to feel regret over the life we didn't have. At this point in my life regret would be foolish and completely unproductive. Nevertheless, at times regret and loss weigh heavy as an anvil on my heart.

I feel these feelings as sharply as though all the events of my life happened last week. How short life is, and how irreversible some things are. We don't know that when we are young. When we are old, it is too late. Or is it?

Yours, C

August 21, 1982

...   .

Local Author Hosts Garden Art Sale to Benefit NOW

Catherine Caldwell, a lifelong Lake Forest resident and author of "The Lake Poet," held a unique memorial on the lawn of her Lake Forest home this past Saturday. Her friend of many years, the journalist and painter Lydia Grinnell, died after a brief bout with cancer in July, and in her will stipulated that her paintings be sold with any proceeds going to benefit the National Organization For Women. It was Ms. Caldwell's idea to hold the sale at her home as a "garden party."

Ms. Caldwell met Ms. Grinnell in the early 1950's when both were assigned to the same shift as ground corpsmen for the Civil Air patrol. "It sounds ludicrous now," remarks Ms. Caldwell, "but at the time we civilians were thought to be an integral part of our country's defense."

The two women remained close friends after their civil air defense duties were over. They were both active members of NOW and the League of Women Voters, and over the years attended many marches and rallies and lectures together for various issues in women's rights.

Ms. Caldwell's husband James Caldwell was the owner of the Forest Inn in Lake Forest, which had been in his family for many years. Shortly after he died in 1975, Lydia Grinnell had an accident and while recovering she moved into Ms. Caldwell's home. Ms. Grinnell, who had a distinguished career as a newspaper reporter in Washington, D. C. before moving to Lake Forest to care for her mother in 1951, never married. She took up painting after deciding to stay in Lake

Forest, and painted oils in an Impressionistic style. Her
favorite locale to paint was Laguna Beach, California, a
mecca for artists since well before the turn of the century.
Several years before her death, Ms. Grinnell bought a home in
Laguna Beach, and she and Ms. Caldwell traveled there during the winters.

Over fifty paintings were removed from their storage place
in the Caldwell attic, and a local gallery owner and art
expert Mr. Arthur Henry was instrumental in cleaning and
framing them, and also determining their monetary value.
"These are charming evocations of both Midwestern prairie
and California desert and ocean," said Mr. Henry. "They
bring to mind the early California Impressionist style of painting, with vivid colors and short, bold strokes."

The showing and sale was attended by hundreds of Lake
Forest and North Shore residents, and also by art dealers from
the Midwest and California. "Lydia's paintings filled my
front and back yard like bouquets of vibrant flowers," said
Catherine Caldwell. "It was a sight she would have loved,
and an image I'll never forget. All these years I tried to get
her to show her work, but she never wanted to. She did it to
please herself, and there was no arguing with her about it."

The benefit showing raised over $45,000 for NOW and its
educational programs.

...   .

January 1, 1984

Dear Sam,

I write from Laguna Beach, once more. Lydia died last
summer. The enclosed news clipping tells a little. She felt a
lump on the side of her throat in the shower one day; it must
have been in May. By July she was gone. So fast. Yet every

day at the time seemed to last a hundred years, because of her pain. It was an awful thing to see.

Lydia left me the beach house here. And I will leave it to the Laguna Art Museum in my own will. Sarah and Rose do visit here sometimes in the winters but they are not attached to California and it wouldn't mean as much to them. Julie comes here with her two little boys once during each winter, but they require all of her attention now, and as much as I know she would like to paint here, she is too distracted to follow through. How well I remember the very real work of family that always comes first.

I'm so very glad to be here, sitting in the sun. The last winter I spent in Lake Forest I thought I would never be warm. Even here I need a sweater all the time, because I easily get a chill from the ocean breeze.

I wish you could have seen the garden party I had for Lydia. The clipping tells it pretty well, although it is a dreadful photo of me. Everywhere you looked, paintings on easels, like I always imagined it would be. Some things in life have a certain inevitability.

Love, C

P. S. Why did it also seem inevitable that Sylvia Plath would win a Pulitzer once her collected poems were put together—after her death? I wonder if the prize would have made her happy or more anxious. Some authors fear prizes, for the pressure they add. How do you top a Pulitzer with your next work?

January 1, 1990

Dearest Sam,

I don't know how long it has been since I last wrote one

of these "secret" letters to you. Several years, I think. I feel
my energy declining, although on some days my heart is the
heart of a young girl. Or my mind remembers how it was,
and my heart follows.

I still write poetry and fill notebooks with images that
come into my head, although I seriously doubt I will ever do
anything with them now. Perhaps some future great grand-
child will have the same leanings as I do, and will be able to
make some sense out of my jottings. I like to think of such a
thing happening.

I've been thinking... There are so few things in the world
that are permanent. Certainly not us mortals; we are the
least permanent of all. Do you think writers and artists prac-
tice their craft in a vain attempt to cheat death? Nice to
think that even though your body and soul have departed
this earth, something of you remains. Art makes us greater
than we are; it connects us to the future. A future we can't
even visualize.

Sitting in the sun on Lydia's Laguna Beach deck I listen
to the singsong voices of my great-grandchildren playing on
the beach, and I am content. So easy now to look back and
second-guess life. But that doesn't really hold meaning. I've
had love and work and family. And I've lost love and family.
Always, though I've had my work.

Fondly, Catherine

January 1, 1995

My dear, dearest heart,

The thing I feared most, more than my own death (which
I no longer fear) was that you would go before me. And without me. Although we really were not without each other. At
all times in my life since I first fell in love with you, you have

been with me in my heart.

I continue to write to you, though, my dearest Sam. If I wouldn't have had that connection in my life to sustain me — this connection of writing to you through the years — I might have led a very lonely life. Whoever reads these letters in the future may judge my life to have been lonely, but a person can never really judge another's choices. For we can never truly know another's heart.

I assume that someone will read these letters some day. And when I return to Lake Forest from Laguna this spring, perhaps for the last time, I will add this letter to the small blue suitcase, with the rest. I have an image in my head that I can't seem to shake. I think I dreamed it, but now it is part of my waking time. Julie rows me out in a small rowboat on Lake Michigan with the letters in the suitcase. It is a beautiful sunny day, and I look back to the shore, where mothers and children are playing on the beach. I remember a day when Bridget and I took the children to the beach. We were all so young, and my Jimmy was there, toddling about on plump legs, running into the water and squealing back out. I can't wait to see Jimmy again.

In the dream I take the suitcase and place it on the water, where it rocks gently with the current. Julie rows me back to the shore and we walk barefoot in the sand to the pavilion. We sit and watch the suitcase, which is just a speck now on the horizon. And then it is gone.

Acknowledgements

I would like to thank the library staff at the Lake Forest Library for their continued encouragement, interest, and support as I waded through nearly seventy years of bound volumes of the *Lake Forester*.

I would also like to thank the staff at Ragdale, an amazing resource for writers and artists, right here in Lake Forest. Their support and encouragement was critical in developing my confidence and my voice. In particular, Sylvia Brown, a director at Ragdale, has been a source of inspiration and good cheer.

Some writer friends have lent invaluable support during this project. Leanne Star was a painstaking editor and gentle critic of this work, and other fiction of mine. Another writer, Alan P. Henry, whose own work is flourishing, has been an enthusiastic cheerleader and good friend from my very first fiction efforts. I am grateful to Shirley Paddock and Janice Hack of the Lake Forest/Lake Bluff Historical Society, and to Dr. Arthur H. Miller, Archivist and Librarian for Special Collections at Lake Forest College, who read with an eye to historical accuracy.

Chris Crosby went above and beyond her duties as a typesetter and designer, and her creative work is gratefully acknowledged. Fine art photographer Robert James Kelly of Lake Forest (robertjkelly.com) was so generous in providing the image for the cover from his incredible collection.

I'm not sure how you thank a whole town for its interest and belief in my work, but I'll try... To all the people who stopped me in Market Square and asked how my book was coming, to the book group leaders who invited me to read my fiction at their meetings, and our two local bookstores: Lake Forest Book Store and B. Dalton's... I am overwhelmed by your encouragement! I hope my love of Lake Forest shows through in these pages.

Andrea Barrett's class at the Bread Loaf Writers' Conference in Middlebury, Vermont in 1997 gave me the push I needed to get my own work "out of the attic."

I am fortunate to have an ever-widening circle of close women friends. I write with our common shared experiences always in mind.

And, as always, these words are for Kelly and Andy, their legacy from their mother. And for Joe, who showed me it could be done my way.

Author's Note

This book is a historical novel, and includes many true events that happened in Lake Forest, and is also set in the context of world events. The characters in this book are fictional, however, use of the real names of people who were a part of Lake Forest history was done as accurately as possible. The Forest Inn is a fictional creation, based on the Deer Path Inn in Lake Forest. The historical events that are associated with the Inn are based on newspaper accounts and other research into the Inn's history.

The following were used in research for *The Lake Poet*:

The *Lake Forester* (1929 – present day) Published now by Pioneer Press, Glenview, Illinois.

Lake Forest, Illinois: History and Reminiscences by Edward Arpee. Published by Lake Forest-Lake Bluff Historical Society, 1991.

Ragdale: A History and Guide by Alice Hayes and Susan Moon. Published by Open Books (Berkeley, CA) and the Ragdale Foundation, 1990.

To read more of Kathy Stevenson's work, please visit www.lakepoet.com. To order additional copies of *The Lake Poet* send $17.25 (includes shipping and handling) to Thirteenth Angel Press   P.O. Box 16   Lake Forest, Illinois 60045. Thirteenth Angel Press does not accept manuscripts or inquiries regarding publication of other materials.

Fitzgerald's Photography

About the Author

Kathy Stevenson's essays, feature articles, and award-winning short stories have appeared in the *Los Angeles Times, Chicago Tribune, The Writer, Redbook, The Christian Science Monitor, American Way, Pioneer Press,* and numerous other national and local publications. She attended the Bread Loaf Writers' Conference in 1997, and has taught writing classes at Ragdale and Gorton Community Center in Lake Forest, Illinois.